*How I spent my summer vacation
by Morgan Brigham, age 29*

Traci and I used to spend every summer together. But that was when we were kids, back when our biggest goal was to see who could stuff more spiders down whose back.

I honestly didn't expect to get stranded with her here today at the old cabin. But now I'm kind of glad. Boy, she sure has changed! This night-alone-in-the-dark is starting to have definite possibilities....

But, of course, I'm not the kind to kiss and tell. And I have a more important mission in mind: I've got to convince her not to marry Dr. Dull. She deserves so much more! She deserves someone who will treat her like an equal; someone who will challenge her, who will keep her life exciting—

Hey! Why does that sound like someone I know?

Dear Reader,

Boy, did Marie Ferrarella's *Traci on the Spot* bring back
a few memories for me. Her heroine is a cartoonist,
and she works out the daily dilemmas of her life via her
character's escapades. I once dated a cartoonist.
However, his character was of the animated-vegetable-
saving-the-world variety, and no way would I have
wanted to be involved in any of *his* escapades. Of
course, maybe if we'd managed to share a night alone
in a romantic cabin, I might have changed my mind.

Our second book this month is *First Date: Honeymoon*,
by Diane Pershing. Mix together one handsome hero
and one waiting-for-Mr.-Right heroine, then add a
sham marriage proposal and an equally ersatz
honeymoon, and voilà! You've got just the right
ingredients for the perfect travel guide to honeymoon
bliss, not to mention passion hot enough to melt
granite and a couple whose next honeymoon is going
to be the very, *very* real variety.

Enjoy both stories, and remember to come back next
month for more adventures in meeting, dating—and
marrying—Mr. Right.

Yours truly,

Leslie Wainger
Senior Editor and Editorial Coordinator

Please address questions and book requests to:
Silhouette Reader Service
U.S.: 3010 Walden Ave., P.O. Box 1325, Buffalo, NY 14269
Canadian: P.O. Box 609, Fort Erie, Ont. L2A 5X3

MARIE FERRARELLA

Traci on the Spot

SILHOUETTE YOURS TRULY™

Published by Silhouette Books
America's Publisher of Contemporary Romance

To all the writers
of the comics
and comic strips
that have fueled my imagination,
brightened my day,
or made me laugh.
Thank you.

SILHOUETTE BOOKS

ISBN 0-373-52039-5

TRACI ON THE SPOT

Copyright © 1997 by Marie Rydzynski-Ferrarella

Illustrations © 1997 by Kim Barnes

About the author

Dearest person who has picked up this book,

All right, I admit it. I'm a cartoonaholic. Cartoons have always fit prominently into my life. I learned how to read by reading wonderful comic books like "Little Lulu" and "Nancy & Sluggo." I progressed to "Superman" (in every single publication that bore his name) and could have majored in super heroes (ask me a question, any question, I dare you). By the time I got my master's degree in Shakespeare (yes, I read comic books through college), I could not only intelligently discuss the bard's plays, but I could also tell you all of the people who figured into Superman's life whose initials were L.L. Even now I feel my day is incomplete without opening the paper and reading the funnies. I love to smile, and if a laugh can be tucked into it, all the better.

That was why writing *Traci on the Spot* was such a kick for me. I could imagine writing a daily comic strip that reflected my life. (Hey, I can deal with pressure—I have two kids, a husband and a German shepherd who thinks she's a lap dog.) I hope Traci (and I) manage to entertain you for a little while.

With love and gratitude,

Marie Ferrarella

Books by Marie Ferrarella

Silhouette Yours Truly
‡The 7lb., 2oz. Valentine
Let's Get Mommy Married
Traci on the Spot

Silhouette Romance
The Gift #588
Five-Alarm Affair #613
Heart to Heart #632
Mother for Hire #686
Borrowed Baby #730
Her Special Angel #744
*The Undoing of Justin
   Starbuck #766*
Man Trouble #815
The Taming of the Teen #839
Father Goose #869
Babies on His Mind #920
The Right Man #932
In Her Own Backyard #947
Her Man Friday #959
Aunt Connie's Wedding #984
†Caution: Baby Ahead #1007
†Mother on the Wing #1026
†Baby Times Two #1037
Father in the Making #1078
The Women in Joe Sullivan's Life #1096
‡Do You Take This Child? #1145
The Man Who Would Be Daddy #1175

Silhouette Special Edition
It Happened One Night #597
A Girl's Best Friend #652
Blessing in Disguise #675
Someone To Talk To #703
World's Greatest Dad #767
Family Matters #832
She Got Her Man #843
Baby in the Middle #892
*Husband: Some Assembly
   Required #931*
Brooding Angel #963
‡Baby's First Christmas #997
Christmas Bride #1069

Silhouette Desire
‡ Husband Optional #988

Silhouette Intimate Moments
*Holding Out for a Hero #496
*Heroes Great and Small #501
*Christmas Every Day #538
Callaghan's Way #601
*Caitlin's Guardian Angel #661
‡Happy New Year—Baby! #686

Silhouette Books
Silhouette Christmas Stories 1992
"The Night Santa Claus Returned"

†Baby's Choice
*Those Sinclairs
‡The Baby of the Month Club

Books by Marie Ferrarella writing as Marie Nicole

Silhouette Desire
Tried and True #112
Buyer Beware #142
Through Laughter and Tears #161
Grand Theft: Heart #182
A Woman of Integrity #197
Country Blue #224
Last Year's Hunk #274
Foxy Lady #315
Chocolate Dreams #346
No Laughing Matter #382

Silhouette Romance
Man Undercover #373
Please Stand By #394
Mine by Write #411
Getting Physical #440

Prologue

◄—►

Morgan Brigham slowly set down his coffee cup on the kitchen table and stared at the comic strip in the center of his paper. It was nestled in among approximately twenty others that were spread out across two pages. But this was the only one he made a point of reading faithfully each morning at breakfast.

This was the only one that mirrored her life.

He read each panel twice, as if he couldn't trust his own eyes. But he could. It was there, in black-and-white.

Morgan folded the paper slowly, thoughtfully, his mind not on his task. So Traci was getting engaged.

The realization gnawed at the lining of his stomach. He hadn't a clue as to why.

He had even less of a clue why he did what he did next.

Abandoning his coffee, now cooling, and the newspaper, and ignoring the fact that this was going to make him late for the office, Morgan went to get a sheet of stationery from the den.

He didn't have much time.

Traci Richardson stared at the last frame she had just drawn. She ran her teeth thoughtfully over her lower lip. Debating, she glanced toward the creature sprawled out on the kitchen floor.

"What do you think, Jeremiah? Too blunt?"

The dog, part bloodhound, part mutt, idly looked up from his rawhide bone at the sound of his name. Jeremiah gave her a look that she felt free to interpret as ambivalent.

"Fine help you are. What if Daniel actually reads this and puts two and two together?"

Not that there was all that much chance that the man who had proposed to her, the very prosperous and busy Dr. Daniel Thane, would actually see the comic strip she drew for a living. Not unless the strip was taped to a bicuspid he was examining.

It wasn't that Daniel belittled the cartoon figure that had begun as a drawing on the bottom of a Christmas card to a childhood friend and evolved into a morning staple that held regular meetings with people over cereal and milk every day in thousands of houses across America. After all, *Traci on the Spot* could be viewed as her alter ego, which, at times, was exactly what she was.

Like now.

But lately, Daniel had gotten so busy he'd stopped reading anything but the morning headlines of the *Times*. His thriving practice had almost doubled in the past year and he was talking about taking on yet another partner.

Still, you never knew. Murphy's Law being what it was, he just might be feeling guilty and make a point of reading her strip.

"I don't want to hurt his feelings," Traci continued, using the dog she had saved from certain execution more than six years ago as a sounding board. She turned in the swivel chair to face the animal. "It's just that Traci is overwhelmed by Donald's proposal and, see, she thinks the ring is going to swallow her up." To prove her point, Traci held up the drawing for the dog to view.

This time, Jeremiah didn't even bother to lift his head.

He was probably used to the sound of her voice droning on in the background, she thought with a sigh.

The advantage of working out of her house was that she wasn't chained to a desk or a clock. She could come and go as she pleased, and if she felt like getting up in the middle of the night and working on a strip in her pajamas, there was no one to tell her not to. The downside was that there wasn't anyone to talk to, to use as a *real* sounding board for her ideas.

Oh, sure, she could always call into the office and talk to Matthew or Jill in the art department. But having to listen to a metallic voice offer her selections from a menu before she could get through to either of them took away some of the spontaneity from the situation.

And she was nothing if not spontaneous.

So why didn't she just jump at this chance to become Mrs. Daniel Thane?

Traci stared moodily at the small velvet box on the corner of her kitchen counter, where it had sat since Daniel had asked her to marry him last Sunday.

She blew out a breath and leaned back so far

in her chair it almost toppled over. Grabbing the edge of the drawing board, she steadied herself, but not before her pens went flying to the floor, a pointed rainbow scattering all over.

Out of the corner of her eye she saw that the sudden commotion had caught the dog's attention. Jeremiah came trotting over to investigate. And to sample.

Traci made a dive for the floor and got to the pens first. "Back. You don't help with the strip, you can't eat a pen."

Gathering them together, she deposited the pens back into the tray. And then studied the last frame again. The Traci character's query fit her quirky nature.

That settled it, she decided. It was going into the paper.

"Daniel isn't going to see it," she told the disinterested dog, more to convince herself than anything else. "He probably won't have time to see any of them."

But Daniel was going to suspect something eventually, she mused.

The very fact that she hadn't grabbed the ring from his hand and slid it onto her finger should have given him a clue that she had doubts about their union.

Traci sighed, dragging both hands through her hair. The blond strands curled around her fingers, momentarily straightening before springing back. What was the matter with her? Daniel Thane was a catch by any definition. A wonderful, kind, loving man who was a doctor, for heaven's sake. Okay, a dentist, but that was almost as good.

So what was her problem?

Her problem, if she were honest with herself, was that she wanted a combination. A mixture of Daniel's stability and kindness and Rory's charm. Rory Conway was an unemployed actor who had been in and out of her life before Daniel had ever entered it.

"Not unemployed," Rory had maintained with alacrity. "Just between jobs." He'd been between jobs for a long while. Longer than they had been together. Rory's main attribute, other than being tall, dark and deadly handsome, was that he could make a woman feel every inch a female in flaming capital letters, from the very tips of her frosted hair down to the edge of her pearl pink polished toes.

And he didn't have a nesting bone in his body.

But Daniel did. All of Daniel leaned toward nesting. Home, hearth, family, that was all he'd talked about this Sunday as she had sat there, holding the velvet box in her numbed fingers, waiting to be struck by that sunny ray of happiness. And waiting and waiting. Daniel said he wanted to take care of her, to fulfill her every whim. And he was even willing to let her think about it before she gave him her answer.

Guilt nibbled at her. She should be dancing up and down, not wavering like a weather vane in a gale. After all, she did love him. Who wouldn't?

But maybe, just maybe, she didn't love him enough.

Still, he was generous, loving and patient. "Can a man get any better than that?" Traci asked aloud.

Jeremiah, having denuded the rawhide bone of its tan color, moaned mournfully in reply.

She waved her hand at him and huffed. "What do you know?"

Pronouncing the strip completed, Traci scribbled her signature in the corner of the last frame and then sighed. Another week's work put to bed. Though she was completely scattered about everything else in her life, when it came to the strip, that was a different matter. There she adhered to schedules and deadlines as if her life, and not just her livelihood, depended on it. It was, at times, as if *Traci on the Spot* reflected her very soul.

"Beats lying on a couch one hour a week," she assured Jeremiah, who couldn't care less. He was settling in for a nice nap in the middle of a warm sunspot pooling on the tile floor.

Very carefully, she slid the strip into her portfolio along with the others she'd completed. That done, she glanced at the pile of mail on the counter. She'd been bringing it in steadily from the mailbox since Monday, but the stack had gotten no farther than her kitchen. She hadn't opened any of it. Most of the envelopes probably contained bills, anyway. Those she allowed to marinate.

The rest were undoubtedly ads and would only

go into the recycle bin. No hurry for that, either. But since she was finished with her work, she thought she might as well make a stab at cleaning, and sorting letters was the least heinous of the annoying chores that faced her.

Traci slid onto the kitchen stool and picked up a handful of mail. She began sorting, tossing envelopes into piles like a dealer at an Atlantic City gambling table.

"Bill, bill," she read, tossing, "ad, petition, pleas for contributions, catalog, bill." It was sad how the bills seemed to outnumber everything else. She shook her head as she continued tossing envelopes onto the uneven piles. "Letter."

Traci paused as she turned the long envelope over. The return address was embossed and in script. Morgan Brigham. Why would Morgan be writing to her? It wasn't Christmas.

Curious, Traci tore open the envelope and quickly scanned the short note inside.

Dear Traci,
I'm putting the summerhouse up for sale. Thought you might want to come up and see it one more time before it goes up on the block. Or make a bid on it yourself. If memory serves, you once said you wanted to buy it. Either way, let me know. My number's on the card.

Take care,
Morgan

P.S. Got a kick out of *Traci on the Spot* this week.

Traci folded the letter, then looked down at the card in her hand. He read her strip. She hadn't known that. A feeling of pride silently coaxed a smile to her lips. She always got that happy-shy reaction when she found out people read *Traci on the Spot*.

After a beat, the rest of his note seeped into her consciousness. He was selling the house.

The summerhouse. A faded white building with brick trim. Suddenly, memories flooded her mind.

Skinny-dipping in the lake when she was five until her mother and her aunt had ordered her and her cousin Adam out of the water. Morgan had told on them. She got even by putting a spider in his bed. He absolutely hated spiders.

Long, lazy afternoons that shone through bright green leaves and felt as if they would never end.

Morgan—his long, lanky body covered with red bumps—biting his lower lip as she applied globs of calamine lotion to his arms and back.

Other memories winked in and out of her mind like fireflies with a mission.

He was going to sell it. Or his parents were. Traci wondered why her mother hadn't told her anything about this. Julia Richardson still remained in touch with Eva Brigham. Friends for thirty years, they lunched together once a month. Talk of the sale must have come up. Why hadn't her mother said anything?

Probably because she'd been screening her

calls and avoiding her mother ever since she'd told her about the engagement ring on Sunday, she thought ruefully.

Traci looked at the far wall in the family room. Part of it was covered with framed photographs from the past. There was a large one of her and Morgan standing before the summerhouse. She couldn't remember which of their mothers had insisted on taking it. She only remembered that both she and Morgan had trouble standing still beside each other long enough for the shot to be taken.

Traci and Morgan. Morgan and Traci. Back then, it seemed their lives had been permanently intertwined. A bittersweet feeling of loss passed over her.

Picking up the card, Traci pulled the telephone over to her on the counter and tapped out the number on the keypad.

"Law Offices," a crisp voice announced after only one ring.

Either business was bad for the firm or someone was awfully efficient, she mused. Who woulda thunk it? Morgan Brigham, a criminal lawyer. "Mr. Morgan Brigham, please."

"Is he expecting this call?" the voice on the other end asked primly.

Traci wound her index finger around the cord as she rocked on the stool. "Absolutely."

It was obvious that the secretary was unconvinced and determined to remain an obstacle. "Whom shall I say is calling?"

She wanted to surprise him. "Why don't you let me tell him that?" Traci suggested stubbornly.

"Madam, this is highly irregular."

Traci wondered if Morgan knew how off-putting his receptionist was. Probably. "I'm nobody's madam, and trust me, he wants this call."

"Well, I—"

The woman abruptly stopped talking. There was the sound of a hand being passed over the receiver and then a muffled exchange of voices in the background. Cradling the receiver between her shoulder and ear, Traci wandered over to the coffeemaker and poured herself a mug. This was going to take a while.

"Hello?" The voice was deep, rich, like the black coffee in her mug.

Startled, Traci paused at the refrigerator, the door opened. "Morgan?"

"Yes?"

She didn't remember his voice being so resonant. It took her a second to collect her thoughts. "This is a voice from your past." Taking out the container of milk, she closed the door with her hip.

"Traci." It wasn't a question, but a statement.

She was a little disappointed that Morgan could guess so easily. It wasn't as if she called him all the time. Or ever.

Pouring, she watched the milk swirl into the darkness. "Yes, how did you know?"

He laughed and the sound seemed to surround her. "You're the only person out of my past who could give my secretary the beginnings of a migraine."

Traci had no idea why that made her smile. "You shouldn't hire such delicate help and you should definitely get yourself a more exciting past."

Obviously, some things never changed, Morgan thought. Traci still had a convoluted way of looking at things. "In order to do that, it would mean that I'd have to work on my present."

Her grin grew. "Yes, it would."

"Still think you know it all, don't you?"

Was that a fond note in his voice or just her imagination? "No, now I know I do. But let's not get into that. I'm holding your note in my hand."

"I was beginning to think you weren't interested. I sent the note out last Friday."

Traci looked at the stack of mail and then at the engagement ring box. She ran the tip of her finger along the lid, then pushed the box back.

"I've been busy."

"So, does that mean you're interested in buying the old place?"

It might do her some good to get away for the day. To get away from the crowds and try to sort out not her mail but her thoughts. Which were in more of a jumbled mess than the stack on her counter.

"I don't know about buying it, but I'd certainly like to look around. When's a good time?"

She heard the rustling of paper, which she assumed was the pages of his calendar.

"How does tomorrow sound?" Morgan asked.
"I don't have to be in court and there's nothing
scheduled I can't push back. Can you get away?"

Tomorrow was Friday and, since she'd finished
the strip, it stood wide open. Daniel wasn't due
back from the convention until late Sunday night.
Traci rustled papers of her own, though hers were
only blank sheets on her drawing board. Funny
how she could feel her competitive nature coming
to the fore just at the sound of Morgan's voice.

"Looks like I can. Noon sound all right?"

He laughed softly. "Still like to sleep in?"

She did, but she didn't see the point in admitting it to him. Knowing him, he'd jump at the
chance to make it sound slothful. "No, I just
don't like driving in the dark and it's roughly a
three-hour trip from where I live."

"All right, I'll meet you there at noon."

That settled, Traci was about to ring off, then
stopped. "Morgan?"

"Yes?"

"Thanks for asking me."

Morgan shrugged it off. "Don't mention it.
You spent as much time there as I did."

"More," she corrected. "You went away to
school, remember?"

He was very quiet on the other end and she
thought for a moment that he hadn't heard her.
Then he answered, "I remember. So I'll see you
at noon tomorrow."

"Bye."

Traci hung up and looked thoughtfully at the

telephone, wondering if she was making a mistake. An uneasiness skated through her, but she attributed it to the decision she had to make.

For a moment, she debated calling Daniel at his hotel and leaving a message for him that she was going to be away. But then she thought better of it. If he knew she was away, he might worry.

No, Daniel never worried. He knew she could take care of herself. He was good like that.

He was good in a lot of ways.

She should have her head examined for even vacillating, she thought, looking at the ring box again. Very carefully she opened it and looked down at the perfectly cut square diamond. It winked and blinked at her, catching the fluorescent light and playing ball with it.

She snapped the lid closed with a shiver.

"No doubt about it. It *does* grow." Putting the box down again, she got ready to take her cartoon strips to the office.

Early the next morning, Traci piled her sketchbook and her dog, along with a well-worn map she never quite got the hang of reading or folding, into her vintage Mustang and drove out of the city.

A sense of excitement and adventure telegraphed itself through her.

Jeremiah had sole possession of the back seat, patrolling the area with the air of a newly liberated king, moving from one window to the other.

Traci had opened each only far enough for him to stick out his nose and only part of his head.

She adjusted her rearview mirror, looking into the back seat as the road threaded onto the expressway. Jeremiah appeared to be one happy dog.

She wished it could be that easy for the rest of the world. "Unfortunately, it takes more than having your ears and tongue flapping in the wind," she said aloud to the dog.

Morning traffic slowly dissipated. It was a long, steady drive. She broke up the monotony by talking to the dog and singing along with the radio. The trip seemed to take longer than she remembered. But then, she'd never made it from the heart of New York City before.

Finally, she was on the last leg. Taking the narrow road off the beaten path, she looked around as she drove in what she hoped was a northeasterly direction. Things looked vaguely familiar, but that could have been wishful thinking on her part. She fervently hoped she wasn't on her way to the Canadian border.

Edginess began to waft through her again. She'd been feeling that way ever since Daniel had given her the ring. Up until that point, she'd been content enough just to float along. Although, at times, that tiny voice that advocated having a husband and children, the one that vaguely resembled her mother's voice, would get a little louder.

What was she doing here, anyway? she demanded silently. Granted, the scenery was tranquil and the ripe autumn colors made it look as if she had tripped and fallen headlong into nature's kaleidoscope. But that should have no bearing on her decision when it came to choosing a partner for life.

For life.

An involuntary shiver shimmied up and down her spine.

Stop it, Traci. He's going to make a great husband.

She knew he would. An excellent, loving husband. Traci thought of Daniel. Dr. Daniel Thane, a man whose blinding smile was the first thing you noticed about him, which was fortunate, given his occupation.

A blinding smile that seemed to lack heart.

Damn it, that wasn't fair. Daniel had heart. He had lots of heart. What he didn't have was chemistry, but so what? There was nothing wrong with being solid, dependable, trustworthy, and Daniel was all those things. He had all the qualities a woman looked for. Her mother loved him.

A feeling like a heavy, rain-soaked blanket fell over her soul. Her mother wasn't going to be married to him; *she* was. For better and for worse.

Forever.

How could one word be so unsettling?

What was the matter with her? She'd had flash and fire and been summarily burned by it when Rory decided to ride off into the sunset. Commitments frightened him the way they seemed to attract Daniel. Rory had abruptly left at the first sign that she wanted to become serious. That was where chemistry got you. With an empty bed and a bruised heart. Daniel wanted to fill her bed and take care of her heart. Forever.

That had to count for something. So he didn't curl her toes; she could live with that. Curled toes were hard to walk on, anyway.

Swerving quickly to avoid a squirrel that had darted out onto the road, she sighed. She wasn't convincing herself. Jeremiah yelped in protest as he tumbled to the side of the car.

"Sorry. You wouldn't want me to hit a squirrel, would you?" The half growl, half whimper behind her had her laughing. She could almost hear what the dog was thinking. "No, you wouldn't. They're too tough to eat."

Slowing down, Traci took a curve, then drove up the winding road slowly.

So what, she thought, picking up the thread of her own internal argument. So what if bells and banjos didn't fill the air when Daniel held her hand or kissed her? Electricity was for the utility company, and for teenagers fumbling in the back seat of a car, not for a grown woman. She would take stability over curled toes any day.

She just wished...

What? Traci thought impatiently, annoyed with the way she was vacillating. She just wished what? That she could feel the wind beneath her sails, to have the sky light up when a man kissed her?

Been there, done that. Gone nowhere.

She should be grateful that Daniel had happened. He'd turned love into a comfortable thing, something she'd just slipped into.

Like clean underwear in the morning.

Traci winced and forced herself to pay attention to the road before she really did hit something. Where *was* that house, anyway?

Traci halted the car abruptly as she stared at the fence up ahead. Was she lost? She didn't remember a fence on the property when her parents had driven up here. And she certainly didn't remember a No Trespassing sign being posted.

There was a tiny M. Brigham in the corner below the declaration.

No, she wasn't lost, Traci decided. The notice had obviously been put up by Morgan. Morgan Brigham had probably grown up to become a pompous ass and his waist had probably thickened while his hair had thinned. Growing up was the pits sometimes.

Traci got out of the car and approached the sign. She ran her hand along it. The last time she'd been here was—when?

Pausing, she linked events up in her mind, searching for a time frame. It had been right before she'd gone away to college. Once college had begun, there just hadn't been enough time to come out here anymore, even though she'd wanted to.

And then her parents had stopped reserving the house for the summer. There seemed to be no point to the time-sharing arrangement anymore.

Their only daughter had grown up and life had taken another road.

Away from here.

For a moment, Traci stood, debating with herself. Something was urging her to turn around and go back. The old adage about not going home again echoed in the corners of her mind. She was afraid that what she would see would shatter the idyllic time childhood had become for her in her mind.

"Coward," she mumbled under her breath.

Unlatching the gate, Traci pulled it open far enough to accommodate her car. Then she got back in and drove up the grassy road.

She could see the house.

Her pulse began to hammer as excitement spilled through her. Yes, that was definitely the house—a two-story, wood-frame building with a chimney that was dwarfed by the trees around it. Just beyond, she knew, was the dock and the lake where she'd learned how to swim. How to kayak. And how to dream.

Without realizing it, she pressed down on the accelerator just as she crossed the wooden bridge.

Traci zoomed over it the way she'd zoomed over so many things in the past few years. Suddenly, she desperately wanted to see the house.

Following the winding path, she traveled the rough, uneven gravel-paved road as far as she could, then pulled the car over to the side. After getting out, she locked it out of habit and went the rest of the way on foot. Jeremiah, eager to stretch his legs after being in the car for so long, fairly galloped down the path. Holding on to the leash, she all but flew behind him.

"C'mon, dog, I don't want to be dragged."

Traci was nearly in front of the door when she heard someone behind her. Alerted, Jeremiah began to bark. And cower.

Cartoonist found dead at house where she spent summers. Film at eleven.

Heart hammering in her throat, vying for space with a gasp, Traci swung around. Her hand was raised up in a pseudo self-defense movement she had absolutely no idea how to execute.

"Took you long enough."

Her mouth fell open. Her hand remained in the air only because it was frozen in place. This drop-dead gorgeous guy just couldn't be—

"Morgan?"

The dark green eyes narrowed within their handsome setting. "None other."

2

His mother was right, Morgan thought as he looked at Traci. Actually, she had understated the matter. She'd said that Traci had grown up to be a ''pretty little thing.'' But she hadn't. Traci Richardson had grown up to be a drop-dead, teeth numbing knockout.

Remembering the strip he'd read today, Morgan glanced down at her left hand. He wasn't too late. Unlike her counterpart, there was no huge diamond winking and blinking on her hand. It was bare.

It was also turning an interesting shade of pink. Red, really. The leash was wrapped around her hand and it was obviously cutting off her circulation. The creature attached to the other end of the leather strap seemed bent on dragging Traci back down to her car.

The dog, for all its size, appeared to be cowering. Morgan couldn't help grinning at the sight as he breathed a little easier. He nodded toward the animal. "Some watchdog you have there."

Traci lifted her chin defensively and took umbrage for the dog. Actually, she thought that when it came to Morgan, she probably would have taken umbrage no matter what he'd said. Their relationship had always taken on antagonistic ramifications whenever they ventured past "hello." It was the nature of the beast, and now that she was older and could look back at her life with a more discerning eye, she had to admit that she rather liked it that way. She'd enjoyed the daily confrontations. They had kept her on her toes and kept her summers from being dull.

Traci glanced at her pet. "Jeremiah does the trick when I need him."

Jeremiah didn't look up to *any* sort of tricks, defensive or otherwise. What the dog did look like was downright sleepy. Even now, his big brown eyes were shutting.

"How?" Morgan asked. "By lying down on the intruder and smothering him to death?"

Blue eyes with flecks of gray narrowed into gleaming slits over the bridge of a very pert nose. "Want a demonstration?"

She'd do it, too, Morgan thought. She'd sic that four-footed monster on him. He wouldn't put anything past her. Morgan held up his hand and laughed. "No, I'll pass, thanks."

Vindicated, Traci loosened her hold on the leash. "Smart move." Eyes moving up and down the length and breadth of him, she sized up a person she'd once known as well as her own reflection. "It would be your first, I imagine."

Same old Traci. In a way, in an ever-changing world, that was almost comforting. Almost.

Morgan nodded. "Seeing as how I invited you up here to look around the old place, I'm inclined to agree with you. At least as far as today goes."

Ready to fire back, Traci opened her mouth, then shut it again. And laughed.

It was that same, skin-tingling, sexy, smoky laugh that he remembered. At the time, it seemed incongruous for a teenage girl to have a laugh like that. But it fit right in with the woman he saw before him. Traci had been a thin, bouncy, perky girl, and while he could still see that in the woman she'd become, there was something a hell of a lot more unsettling about the way she looked at him now than there had been then.

And even then, the sound and the occasional look had gotten to him, although Morgan would have willingly swallowed his own tongue before admitting it to her or anyone else.

"Well, I see you haven't changed any," Traci told him.

At least, she amended silently, his attitude hadn't. Looks-wise, well, that was a whole other story. Her mother had told her that he was good-looking, but mothers were obligated to say things like that about their best friends' sons. It was a rule that was written in stone somewhere or other.

Who would have thought that, for once, it was actually true?

In response, Morgan made an exaggerated show of looking down at himself, as if to check out what she was saying. In his opinion, he'd changed a hell of a lot, and they both knew it. He had a well-worn, banged-up set of weights housed in his garage that he had exercised with daily for the past eight years to prove it.

"I was a lot skinnier the last time you saw me. I've put on a few pounds."

And magnificently well, too, she thought. But if he expected her to admit that, he was going to be sadly disappointed.

"I noticed," she murmured. She suddenly jerked to attention as Jeremiah yanked hard on the leash. It felt as if her left hand had lengthened by a good inch. "Jeremiah, stop that."

To reinforce the command, Traci gave the leash

a good, solid tug. The dog responded by yanking even harder on his end.

Unprepared, Traci gasped, stumbled and then fell unceremoniously into Morgan's arms. The unexpected weight made him fall backward. Breaking her fall, he landed with a hard thud against some very hard upstate New York earth. The pain was temporarily muted by the fact that Traci, and every single curve she possessed, was on top of him.

Traci was more than vaguely aware that the contours melding with hers were infinitely pleasing. More than that, she felt a warm rush spreading fast and furious through every pulsing inch of her body, like a backdraft bent on eating its way through a building in record time.

The overwhelming sensation made her suck in her breath in surprise. If she hadn't known better, she would have said she was on fire.

And maybe, just maybe—in a very unnerving way—she was.

The slow, lazy smile that drifted across Morgan's lips, filtering down from his green eyes and settling in the dimple at the corner of his mouth told her that he was not unaware of what was happening here.

On the contrary, he seemed very, very aware that their bodies were fitting together like two missing pieces of a puzzle.

There was a catch in her throat she didn't like. A catch that *wasn't* there when she was in the same sort of position with Daniel. Of course, she'd never had the wind knocked out of her by Daniel, she argued with herself.

Maybe that was just the trouble.

She'd gotten softer than he remembered, Morgan thought, and yet she was firm. Ripe for the touch. He found himself wanting to gather some very vital, hands-on experience.

To placate himself, Morgan raised his hand to her hair and lightly combed his fingers through it. "I see you have your dog well trained."

Nope, she definitely didn't care for this feeling zipping through her. Traci scrambled up, purposely driving an elbow into his chest as she gained her feet.

"You frightened him," she accused, grabbing at the first defense she could think of. Lame at best, she admitted silently. But then, she wasn't feeling very witty at the moment. Just disoriented.

It took Morgan a moment to catch his breath. Her elbow, sharply applied to his solar plexus, had temporarily siphoned off his air. No doubt about it, he thought. Traci was still quick with her hands and her tongue. In an odd sort of way, that left him with a rather pleasant sensation.

The cards they exchanged at Christmas were basically the typical kind, saying very little, just keeping old lines open much the way occasionally flipping through a dusty family album kept old memories alive. But it didn't fill in any of the missing gaps that were occurring as time passed.

Morgan had learned more about her life from her strip than he had from the cards she'd sent him over the years. It gave him a window into her world that she didn't have into his, he thought. That, too, pleased him. He'd always liked being one up on her.

Drawing his feet to him, Morgan rose and dusted himself off. She looked a little frazzled, he noted. It was a good look on her.

He looked cute with his hair mussed, she mused, then immediately upbraided herself for it. And him for putting the thought into her head in the first place.

"Nothing broken?" she asked solicitously.

He was glad the storm that had been threatening hadn't hit yet. Otherwise, he would have found himself caked in mud. "No."

Traci shook her head. "Damn."

He had to look to see if she was serious. The Traci he remembered would have been. She was always bent on one-upmanship and getting the better of him. They had that in common, he mused. He would have said she was a she-devil if there hadn't been moments when a kinder nature had broken through.

But those moments were few and far between, more of an aberration than anything else. He told himself that he always breathed a little easier when he wasn't around her.

Still, Traci had fluttered along the perimeter of his mind all these years like a tune he couldn't get rid of but couldn't remember all the words to, either. That was Traci all over. Too annoying, too unsettling, to forget. Ever.

He realized he was staring at her and cleared his throat, mentally getting his bearings. "So, you want to see the house or not?"

There was an awkwardness between them, she realized. Beneath the light sparring, there was something she couldn't quite pinpoint. She wondered if time had done that to them or if there was another cause behind it.

"I'm here," she reminded him needlessly.

His eyes washed over her, taking full measure. Boy, but she had filled out. Her blond hair was still as unruly as ever, giving her a moppet look, but the moppet had a figure that made a man's mouth water and his hands grow suddenly restless. Like the rest of him.

"Yes, you certainly are." He took a deep breath and tried to place the scent that had been driving him crazy since she'd landed on top of him. "Sin?"

Traci stared at him, uncomprehending. "Excuse me?"

The surprised look on her face had him wondering if she thought he was propositioning her.

"The perfume you're wearing, is it Sin?"

It took her a minute to put the two pieces of information together. He was looking at her the way she wasn't accustomed to being looked at, not by him, at any rate.

"Oh, yes, it is." She hated this awkward feeling. To counteract it, she was purposely sarcastic. "Good nose. Is that part of your skills as a lawyer?"

He was probably going to hear a hell of a lot of lawyer jokes before this visit was over, he thought. "No, Cynthia favored it."

"Cynthia?" Traci frowned, rolling the name over her tongue. "Is there a Cynthia?"

Was there ever, but that, mercifully, was in his past. Every man was entitled to one Cynthia. One damn mistake in judgment. "There was."

Traci paused. There was a note of sadness in his voice, and something more. For a second, compassion filled her. And then she remembered. Compassion went out the window.

"Wasn't that the girl who used to hang on your arm, simpering all the time?"

She had hated Cynthia Fairling from the first moment she laid eyes on her. Morgan had brought her out the summer Traci was sixteen. The last summer he was here. Delicate, curvy and china-doll perfect, Cynthia had had Traci constructing dolls out of rolled tissues and sticking pins into them in her room. She hadn't realized then that she'd created the voodoo dolls out of jealousy. She did now.

"She didn't—" Morgan thought better of his protest. There was no point in denying the truth. "Well, maybe she did at that."

Maybe? "She most certainly did." Traci fluttered her lashes and hooked her arm around his. She almost hung from it as she pushed her chest forward, mimicking Cynthia to a tee. "Oh, Morgie, that's so clever."

Morgan had the good grace to wince at the imitation. "Ouch."

Traci sighed and shook her head in disapproval as she released him. "I can't believe you let anyone call you Morgie."

Morgan shrugged. "I was eighteen and she was a knockout."

Traci's frowned deepened. Men were so shallow, it was a wonder they survived as a race at all. "You were an idiot and she was out for your money."

He thought back to the way Cynthia had dumped him without warning when he had told her about his father's finances taking a sharp nosedive because of a series of bad investments. It had been a hell of a rude awakening for him on more than one level. He'd learned what it was like to go out and earn his own money quickly enough. It had taken him five years to get through his undergraduate studies, but the degree had meant more to him in the end.

And so had losing Cynthia. It was only at the end that he realized how narrow his escape had really been.

"You had that right." He laughed shortly. "She really was out for my money. How did you know?"

Traci rolled her eyes. "Oh, please, she was transparent."

Not to him. But he allowed Traci her moment of triumph. "Even to a sixteen year old?"

Traci let out a short, exasperated breath. "Even to a mushroom."

The dried, brown leaves crunched beneath the heels of his new boots as he led the way to the front door. "Doesn't say much for me, does it?"

"Nope."

For a second, she wanted to rub his nose in it. She could have told him what Cynthia was all about from the start, but he wouldn't have wanted to listen. He was completely besotted with her. Traci had been angry and hurt when all of his attention had gone to the pretentious little witch. But he'd learned the hard way and, in a way, Traci did feel bad for him.

After a beat, Traci relented. "I guess all men are a little blind when they're being played up to."

He stopped at the front door, his hand on the knob. She was sounding a little too highhanded for his taste. "And you're an expert on this?"

"I see things. I have to," she added deliberately, adding one more log to the fire that was about to catch.

Morgan nodded sagely, as if taking every word as gospel. "That would be the tremendous insight you have into life as a cartoonist, I take it."

She saw the way he was poking his tongue in his cheek. She could endure a lot, but she didn't like having her strip ridiculed. "Did you invite me out here to argue with you?"

She was right. There was just something about having her around that turned him into a competitive adolescent. Something he hadn't been for quite some time.

"No, I invited you to take a last look around. Truce?" To back up his words, Morgan put his hand out to her.

Jeremiah immediately began barking again. The fur on the animal's back stood up as straight as it could, given the shortness of his coat. Morgan wondered uneasily if the dog was all bark and no bite. He certainly hoped so, but since it was Traci's dog, he wasn't placing any bets yet.

"Truce."

Traci placed her hand into his. His handshake was firm, warm. But for some reason, she felt as if, somewhere, a bell was ringing, signaling the beginning of another round.

She glanced over her shoulder. "Jeremiah, quiet!" she ordered. The look she gave the dog was far more effective than her words. The dog lowered his head and looked almost contrite.

"Impressive."

Traci grinned in response. The years melted away and she looked fifteen again, he thought. There was mischief in her eyes.

He opened the door and she began to follow him inside. Morgan placed a restraining hand on her shoulder. He nodded behind her. "Is he coming in, too?"

An amused brow arched. Was he afraid of Jeremiah? "Don't worry, he's housebroken."

"I don't like the emphasis on the word *broken*."

Her smoky laugh surrounded him.

"Trust me." Traci glanced up at the sky. Since she had arrived, the dark clouds had moved in, blotting out the sun and any blue that had been noticeable. "Besides, it might rain any minute. I don't want him getting wet." Jeremiah smelled absolutely atrocious when he was wet, but she refrained from mentioning that.

"Maybe he'll shrink," Morgan commented.

She looked at Morgan in surprise. "You've gotten a sense of humor. Where did you find it?"

He graciously put up with her dig and countered. "I always had it. I had to, spending summers out here with you around."

She shrugged, finally walking into the house. "You never displayed it before."

Any other words faded away as she looked around the large front room. It was dusty and unused, and sad because of it. It was a place meant for laughter and long summer nights shared with friends and family. If she tried hard, she could almost see past summers spent here.

Waves of yesterday surrounded her as the scent of wood from the woodpile by the fireplace wafted to her. The house smelled dank and musty.

And wonderful for all that.

She'd forgotten how much she enjoyed coming here. How much she missed it.

It was yesterday again. And yet an eternity seemed to separate her from that carefree, mischievous girl she'd been.

Morgan stood by, silently letting her reacquaint

herself with the room. He'd journeyed down his own memory lane earlier. It was odd how sentimental you could get about a place that hadn't meant anything to you at the time.

"It hasn't changed much," she commented slowly, the words drifting from her lips.

Even the old television set in the corner was there. With rabbit ears, she thought fondly. Reception had always been miserably poor. It had been her main complaint about vacationing here. Tired of her complaints, her mother had urged her to use her imagination to entertain herself rather than an electronic baby-sitter. Traci had complied by finding new ways to get under Morgan's skin.

"Not down here," Morgan agreed. He began leading the way out of the room, uneasily keeping one eye on the dog. Jeremiah was investigating the multicolored throw rug in front of the fireplace, sniffing so hard he looked as if he were going to absorb the material through his nose. "They redid the bedrooms a few years back. And the attic seems more crammed—"

Traci looked at Morgan sharply. "The bedrooms? My room? They redecorated my room?"

The possessive note surprised him, but then it shouldn't have, he thought. She was always possessive about things she laid her hands on. They spent an entire summer arguing over who got to use the kayak. She usually won.

"Technically, it wasn't your room, it was—"

"My room, Counselor," Traci interjected. "It was always my room in the summer." She was already heading for the stairs, eager to see it. "I don't care what it was the rest of the time. Can I see it?"

"Sure. This way." Hurrying, Morgan got in front of her. Jeremiah, he noted gratefully, had decided to rest on top of the rug he had all but inhaled. He felt along the wall for the light switch. "I had the electricity turned on so I could show the house to its best advantage."

Quickening her step, she passed Morgan and reached the stairs first. She laid a hand on the banister, Columbus claiming the new land for the queen. "You don't have to show me."

He raised his hand, making a show of backing off. "Sorry, habit."

Foot planted on the first step, Traci turned and looked at him, amused. "You're a tour guide on the side?"

"No, I'm used to being polite." The staircase was steep and narrow. It wasn't meant to accommodate two. He joined her, anyway, standing stubbornly on the first step. The fit was tight. "Something you probably are unfamiliar with."

There it was again, that tingling sensation as if a thousand fireflies were holding a convention along her skin. It came when he was brushed up against her. Traci struggled hard to ignore it. "When it comes to you, yes."

He looked down into her face and marveled at the blueness of her eyes. Had they always been that intense? "Does it give you pleasure, bickering with me every chance you get?"

"Infinite pleasure." It wasn't easy, remembering the train of her thought. The tracks were leading toward some very unfamiliar ground. "And this is the first chance I've gotten in years, remember?"

"Yeah." The word stretched out as the smile took hold of his lips and spread. "Maybe we should have done this more often."

She didn't care for the arrhythmic beating of her heart.

"You're the one who went off to college with Cynthia," she said the name in a singsong tone, "and got too busy to come back to the lake." That sounded too much like an accusation, she thought, but it was too late to take it back. Any protest would have him thinking things that weren't true.

With a huff, she pushed past Morgan and walked up the stairs ahead of him.

"You weren't far behind," he countered. "Valedictorian."

Surprised, she turned and looked at him again. "I never wrote you that."

"Didn't have to." He urged her on with a motion of his hand. He was in no hurry to have his systems scrambled again. "My mother made sure I got word." He didn't add that, at times, he prodded his mother for information in what he told himself was just idle curiosity.

"Mothers." The single word spoke volumes. "They can be a network all their own."

"Yeah, they can." At the landing, he followed

her down the hall to her room. It was the last one in a row and the first to get the morning light.

Morgan allowed her to open the door, seeing as how she thought of the room as her own. "Speaking of which, does she ever take offense?"

Traci stopped just short of the threshold. "Who?"

"Your mother."

Turning around, she looked at him, perplexed. "Take offense to what?"

Morgan remembered a recent cartoon that had been less than flattering. "At the way you portray her sometimes in the strip."

Traci waved that aside. "That's not my mother. That's a composite."

That might be what she told others, but he knew better. And he knew her mother, or had. "Is that what you tell her?"

Traci couldn't help the grin that slipped out. "Yeah."

Morgan nodded solemnly, but his eyes were glinting. "And she buys it?"

"Pretty much." Traci grew serious. "Besides, it's all in fun and the traits are exaggerated."

Morgan folded his arms before him as he leaned against the wall, studying her. He could always tell when she was lying. "But it is your life."

"Hey, writers always draw on what they know." She played the words back in her head when he grinned at her. "No pun intended."

He felt as if he'd been watching her life for the past three years. For the most part, it had been amusing. Like Traci. But now, something serious was about to take place. Something he'd found himself not quite ready or willing to accept. "So, are congratulations in order?"

He'd acquired an unnerving way of skipping around conversations since she'd last spoken to him. "What do you mean?"

"Your engagement. To the doctor."

"Dentist," she corrected. "And I'm not."

"Oh?" he asked a tad too innocently. "I thought he gave you a ring."

She wondered if he had picked that up from the strip, or if her mother had told his. "He did. I just haven't given him an answer yet."

That was interesting, he thought. Very interesting. "I see."

She had no idea what he thought he "saw," but she knew what she wanted to see. Her room.

"I doubt it." Turning her back on him, Traci opened the door and stepped into the small guest room.

I HAVE _GOT_ TO STOP SAYING "FOREVER"!

3

"You got rid of the bureau."

Traci went straight toward the new piece of furniture that stood in its stead and looked at it as if it were an intruder. If she tried hard, she could visualize the old one—a honey-colored triplechested bureau that gave the room a crammed, homey quality. Coupled with her double bed, it had turned the place into her own tiny kingdom when she had been growing up. The new bureau was sleeker and took up far less space.

She hated it on principle.

Morgan followed her into the room and shrugged casually. "It was old."

That was the beauty of it, but she doubted if Morgan could understand. Sighing over the loss, Traci ran her fingertip along the dark wood.

"It had a dent in it, right here." She rested her finger on the uppermost corner closest to him. "Where you chipped your tooth."

He remembered the incident vividly. His manhood had been shaken that day. Thin and wiry, two years younger, Traci had easily gotten the best of him. He'd persuaded his parents to buy him his first set of weights that autumn.

"Where *you* chipped my front tooth," he corrected. He knocked against the side in a rapid tattoo. "Somehow, my parents didn't think refurbishing the bureau was a high priority." The bureau was fairly falling apart when they had finally gotten rid of it.

Traci shifted her attention from the bureau to Morgan. She'd completely forgotten about his chipped tooth until this moment.

"Let me see," she said suddenly, catching him off guard.

As he stared at her, Traci placed her thumb on the edge of his chin and pulled down lightly with the familiarity of a maiden aunt or annoying sibling. Or the girl he had partially grown up with.

She nodded at the gleaming white crown. If she hadn't known which one was chipped, she wouldn't have been able to guess which was the false tooth.

"Nice job."

Morgan pulled his head back. "In case you haven't noticed, I'm not a thoroughbred whose teeth you can check out."

The choice of words tickled her. "Thoroughbred?" Traci echoed. "If I was passing out labels, I would have said an old firehouse plug."

She crossed to the bed. By the way it sagged slightly in the middle she could tell it was the same one she'd slept on all those hot summer nights. If Morgan hadn't been in the room, she would have jumped on it for old times' sake.

"Firehouse plug?" He laughed. Who talked like that anymore? "You're dating yourself."

She glanced at him, bemused at the way he was watching her. Was he expecting her to do something weird? "I'm dating my research."

With Traci, it was always difficult to tell if she was being flippant or sincere. He had a fifty-fifty chance of guessing right. "Is that how you met?"

The view from her window was as stirring as she remembered. But the lake looked as if it was going to be blotted out at any minute by the dark clouds that were rolling over it with the intensity of an oncoming express train.

"Who?" she asked, preoccupied.

"You and the dentist?"

She turned around slowly and looked at Morgan. It took her a moment to make sense of his words. She couldn't read his expression. What was he up to?

"No, and his name is Daniel. I meant I was giving a date *to* my research." She touched the curtains. They were the same. Light, filmy. They suited the room, and now, ultimately, her. They hadn't when she was younger. She'd been a tomboy through and through when they'd first begun to take their vacations here and had jeered at the curtains and blue eyelet comforter. "I'm watching old cartoons—"

He could see her, Morgan thought. Sitting curled up on the sofa with a bowl of popcorn in her lap, fascinated by silly little animated characters doing absurd, impossible things in the space of seven minutes. It was a scene directly out of his past, one he'd ridiculed countless times.

Now it just made him feel oddly nostalgic.

"Aren't you afraid they're above you?"

She purposely ignored him. Idly, she opened the nightstand drawer. A spider skittered away, vainly seeking sanctuary. She shut the drawer again. Traci didn't know what she expected to find, maybe a memento from years gone by...

"To see what made some of them special and gave them longevity," she finished, her teeth clenched. "You are as irritating as ever."

He laughed at the expression on her face. His answer held no malice. "Right back at you."

"'Right back at you'?" she repeated incredulously. "A Harvard graduate and that's the best you can do?" Traci shook her head. "Boy, they must have really lowered their standards for you."

They both knew that he'd been an honor student in high school. His studiousness was one of the things she'd used as ammunition when she teased him.

"It was Yale," he corrected patiently, "and the standards were quite high." His eyes washed over her. He wondered if this Daniel character knew what he was letting himself in for. And if he deserved her. "It seems that every time I'm with you, I regress."

She couldn't resist reaching up and mussing his too-perfect hair. "Or loosen up."

Morgan ran both hands through his hair, attempting to smooth it back down. "Trust me, no one wants to be that loose."

Made no difference to her. "Have it your own way. You don't know what you're missing."

Traci ran her hand over the new bureau again. It felt too sleek to her, too benign and devoid of character. The old one had had nicks and scrapes awarded by time all over its surface. Some of the nicks, of course, had been awarded by her.

She smiled to herself, remembering, feeling the room's ambience. For a moment, Traci closed her eyes, letting it all return to her. She'd been five when they had started coming out here. Or maybe even four, she wasn't sure.

Standing in her old bedroom now, feeling the years all melting away, it was as if nothing had really changed. But of course it had. She'd grown up and so had Morgan. An awful lot.

He watched the way her lashes, so much darker than her hair, swept along the swell of her cheeks, resting there like silken kittens reposing on a satiny cushion.

And wouldn't she laugh if he voiced that thought aloud, he thought to himself. Traci was far too earthy to stand still for sentiments like that.

"What are you doing?" he asked.

Her eyes remained closed. "Remembering." And then they fluttered open and she turned them on him. "Whatever happened to her?"

"Who?" Morgan was thoroughly convinced that there were short circuits throughout the entire surface of her brain. How else could she possibly think her disjointed statements made any sense?

"Miss Shallow of 1985." When Morgan still didn't seem to comprehend, Traci batted her lashes at him coquettishly. "Cynthia."

He really didn't feel like discussing Cynthia any further. She was a mistake he wanted to leave buried in his past. A mistake that had made him hesitant to put his heart up on the block again.

"She found someone else. With more money." He stood with his hand on the knob, impatience creasing his brow. "Are you done in here?"

He wasn't impatient with her, Traci thought, but with the subject. It didn't take a rocket scientist to see that.

"Not yet." She paused. Though she didn't often admit it, even to herself, there was a small, soft spot in her heart when it came to Morgan. After all, he was rather like the big brother she'd never had and, while they might fight constantly, she didn't like the idea of anyone else hurting him, no matter what she might profess verbally to the contrary.

Traci placed her hand on his arm. It felt hard to the touch. She ran the tip of her tongue along her upper lip before she managed to force the words out. "I'm sorry."

She was, he thought. He could see it in her eyes. The last thing in the world he wanted was pity, especially hers. That wasn't what they were all about, he and Traci. It added a dimension he didn't want.

"About what?" he asked a little too innocently. "You've got so much to be sorry about, you're going to have to narrow that down a little for me."

She stiffened, dropping her hand. That's what she got for being nice to Morgan. "I was going to say about Cynthia, but—"

He relented. There was no point in closing off this new avenue between them. It just might lead somewhere. "You were?"

Too late to take her words back now, she thought. "Yes." The admission came grudgingly.

Morgan studied her face, trying to ascertain a reason for this change in attitude. He failed.

"Why?"

She shrugged. She'd never cared for having to explain herself. And feelings were a great deal harder to explain than anything else. "I don't like seeing people get hurt."

That might be true enough, but he wasn't "people." He was Morgan. Someone she had taken delight in teasing and torturing. She was throwing away a perfect opportunity to crow and say "I told you so" in every way available to her. It wasn't like her.

"I would have thought the idea would have made you overjoyed, seeing it was me."

For a moment, she stood and looked at him, seeing both the boy she'd known and the man she merely assumed she knew. Maybe they both deserved the truth. Although they both probably wouldn't understand. Men rarely did. She'd learned that one the hard way.

"No, I can rag on you all I want, but that doesn't mean I want to see your heart pierced with a lance. She really didn't deserve you, you know." Traci bit her lip. The last sentence had just slipped out.

His eyes narrowed. She couldn't have surprised him more than if she'd announced that she was harboring a secret crush on him all these years.

"Are you being nice or is there a hidden barb in there that I'm missing?"

She let out a long sigh. *Cast ye pearls before swine*... "I'm being nice," she snapped. And then her sense of humor returned. "Don't blink or you'll miss it."

Something small and warm stirred within him. "I won't."

Ushering her out of the room, Morgan closed the door behind them. Even so, he could hear the wind picking up, mourning low like a choir beginning to rehearse a rousing spiritual. He hoped the storm would hold off until the night.

"Want some coffee?" he offered. "I just put some up before you arrived."

"I'd love some. There's a real chill in the air." Almost reflexively, she ran her hands up and down her arms. The thin sweater she was wearing wasn't nearly warm enough to ward off the cool turn of the weather. "It was always so hot whenever we were out here."

He followed her down the stairs, enjoying the gentle sway of her hips. She had certainly filled out since he last saw her. Something about being a late bloomer stuck in his mind. It was a phrase his mother liked to use. He'd never understood it until now.

"That's because you just spent summers here," he reminded her.

Traci stopped at the landing and turned toward him. "Did you ever come out any other time?" It had never occurred to her that he might have.

He nodded. "A couple." The look in her eyes told him she wanted details, so he stopped to consider. "Once for Thanksgiving. And then once over the Christmas holidays." That time he remembered more vividly. It was actually the last time he'd been here, until this month. "Mother and Dad were in Europe that year." A thin, humorless smile curved his mouth. "One final hurrah before tightening their belts."

Once in the kitchen, Traci crossed to the cupboard where the dishes had always been kept. It surprised her to find only a few pieces left. But then, of course there wouldn't be many. No one stayed here anymore.

She took down two mugs, rinsed them out and then set them on the counter beside the coffeemaker.

"And you were here alone?"

He might have known she'd probe. "No, not quite alone."

"Oh." Something in his voice had alerted her. "Cynthia?" She knew the answer to that would be yes before he said anything. She just didn't know why it bothered her so much.

It was easier answering Traci with his back to her. "Yes. That was when I asked her to marry me."

"You actually—" She hadn't known that it had gone that far. Maybe because she'd refused to think about Morgan and Cynthia together in any more intimate a situation than sitting beside each other on the dock. Traci realized that her mouth had dropped open. "Well, your bad taste was your business, I guess. I take it she turned you down."

That must have stung. Compassion stirred again within her.

He took two spoons out of the drawer and then

shoved it closed a little harder than he intended. Feelings long dead resurfaced and did a little war dance within him.

"Not at first." Morgan turned around. "At first she said yes. It was when she was planning our life together in very lavish terms that I told her about Dad and what the stock market had done to his investments."

Traci knew that the Brighams' financial woes had begun in October. That left a gap of two months.

"You hadn't told her until then?"

He slowly shook his head. Morgan remembered rehearsing in the mirror the way he would break the news to Cynthia. Stupid way for a man to behave. He'd never felt that unsure of himself again. "It wasn't something you wanted to take out an ad about."

She didn't understand. "But this was the kind of thing you would share with someone you were close to."

Morgan shrugged again. In typical blunt fashion, Traci had gotten to the crux of it. "Maybe that was the trouble. Maybe I was never really that close to her." He sighed, remembering the way moonlight caught in Cynthia's hair. Hell of a criterion to pick a bride by. "Just dazzled and wildly enamored."

Enamored? "God, I haven't heard anyone talk like that since—" Traci's mouth curved. "The last time I was here with you."

Morgan's story only confirmed her own argu-

ment that she should be overjoyed at finding
someone as steady, as dependable and loving, as
Daniel. Look what being head over heels got you.
Nothing but disappointment.

There, that settled it. She'd made up her mind.

But her heart...

Morgan took no offense at her words. Lifting
the coffeepot, he took it off the hot plate and
brought it over to the table.

"Still take it with a ton of cream?" he asked,
pouring the dark liquid into her mug. He placed
the carton of cream in front of her.

He took his black. Had he bought this especially for her? The thoughtfulness behind the
small action surprised and pleased her.

Traci nodded. "And sugar."

Morgan filled his own mug, then set the pot
down. He still had a few packets of sugar in his
pocket from when he'd gotten a container of coffee at the diner. Digging them out, he tossed the
white packets on the table beside her mug.

"This is all I have. I forgot about the way you
liked to rot your teeth."

She tore open one envelope, then another.
White crystals rained into the mug. "Hey, I still
have all of mine."

He shook out one for himself. "Mine didn't
rot," he reminded her. "It was punched out."

"Not technically," she was quick to retaliate.
"I hit you in the stomach. *You* were the one who
hit your mouth on the bureau."

She remembered how frightened she'd been

when she'd seen all that blood. Morgan had been teasing her and she'd only meant to get him out of her room, not maim him. He'd surprised her when he'd taken the blame and told his parents that he'd tripped on the scatter rug in her room. She'd never been able to figure out why he had passed up that perfect opportunity to get back at her. It was almost chivalrous.

Maybe that tiny, warm spot in her heart for him had been created that day.

Mug cupped in his hands, Morgan regarded her quietly. "You would have made a hell of a lawyer, you know that?"

Since he was one himself, she took it as a compliment. And returned it in kind. Remembering the incident had her feeling rather magnanimous toward him. "You were the one who kept me sharp."

"I take no credit for that. You were born sharp. With a sharp tongue to match. Hell, you were probably born talking."

He was one to throw rocks. She lifted her chin slightly. "I'm not the one who could talk the ears off a brass monkey."

"No," he admitted agreeably, then his eyes crinkled with a smile. "But you're the one who could make the monkey run off, holding his ears and screaming."

Just like old times. Traci grinned at Morgan over the rim of her mug. A cozy feeling nestled in her chest. "Nice to know nothing's changed."

There he had to disagree. Again. A whole

world had changed since they had sat here like this the last time. "But it has. We're older. Reasonably successful—"

"Not to hear your mother talk about it."

He knew what she meant. His mother heralded every win in court as if he had just single-handedly preserved justice. "Or yours."

The wind was definitely getting louder. She took another sip of her coffee. The extra shot of warmth fortified her. "I guess they have a one-upmanship of their own going on."

There, at least, they were in agreement. But it was a friendly sort of thing between their mothers. Not like between them. He thought of the way they had taken an instant dislike to each other, much to their parents' dismay. "I think we really disappointed them."

She set her mug down and leaned forward. Even in the fading light, his eyes were intensely green, she mused. "How so?"

She was so close, he felt an overwhelming urge to touch his mouth to hers. The thought startled him. Morgan stared down into his almost empty mug. "I think they saw us winding up together."

Traci laughed, grateful she wasn't drinking at the time. She would have choked. She sincerely doubted that her mother had ever thought of the two of them as a couple. Julia Richardson was far more perceptive than that.

"Not if they were looking."

Fragments of a dozen different memories

flashed through his mind. "I guess that does sound pretty crazy."

She didn't quite like the way he said that. "Yeah, thinking I'd settle for you."

There it was again, that superior tone of hers. *That* hadn't changed in more than twenty years. "I was thinking of it the other way around."

She sniffed and looked away. "You would."

His eyes narrowed. For a second, he was fifteen again. And she was thirteen. An annoying, bratty, know-it-all thirteen. "Yes, I would."

This time when she leaned across the table, her eyes were flashing. "What makes you think I'd want to be with you?"

He rose in his chair, inch for inch. "What makes you think I'd want to be with you?"

She waved her hand carelessly at him. "Nothing, except that for once you'd have shown more taste than to go mooning after a money-grasping Barbie doll."

All right, since she'd chosen to go down this path again, he'd call the shots. "And you've done better with your dentist?"

He surprised her. It wasn't like him to fight dirty. That was her domain. "You leave Daniel out of this. You don't know anything about him."

Bull's-eye. He'd gotten to her, he thought with a touch of smugness. He savored the tiny victory. "Word gets around. Your mother told my mother."

That didn't make any sense. Anything her

mother would have said would have been rose-colored. "My mother adores Daniel."

That might very well be true. When Morgan had called his mother last Friday, as soon as he'd read the cartoon, he'd been told that the man was practically sterling. But Morgan had also read between the platitudes.

"From the description I got, your intended is as lackluster as liver."

Traci rose to her feet so quickly the chair almost fell over. She grabbed for it before it could crash to the side. Incensed, she came to Daniel's rescue. "He is not. He's an exciting, vibrant man."

Morgan wondered if Traci was trying to convince him, or herself. In either case, she wasn't succeeding. He could see it in her eyes. "So, why are you having doubts?"

Everything about her body language reminded him of a soldier preparing for battle.

"I am not having doubts," she lied.

The higher her voice rose, the lower, calmer, his became. "Then why aren't you wearing his ring?" A knowing smile took over. "Afraid a squirrel will mug you out here?"

She said the first thing that popped into her head. "It's too big for me to wear." She realized her mistake the moment the words were out.

He looked at her knowingly. She thought she saw compassion in his eyes and could have spit. "Yes, I read the strip this morning."

Flattery took a back seat to indignation for

Daniel. "I told you, everything there is an exaggeration. I take liberties with things," she insisted with more passion than she intended. "Otherwise, they're not funny."

He'd forgotten how magnificent anger made her. Or maybe he'd never really noticed. He did now. "You know what's funny? You settling for comfortable and complacent."

Was he comparing Daniel to himself? She wasn't sure, but she took a stab at it, anyway. "Comfortable and complacent doesn't give me a headache, and what would you know about what I want in a man?" His presumption galled her.

"Educated guess," he answered calmly. "You'd want someone to send your temperature soaring, to keep you on your toes." He hadn't meant to use her own description of him. That had been an accident. He hoped she was too fired up to notice.

"Shows how much you know. Daniel is mentally stimulating enough, thank you." She dragged a hand through her hair. "Look, maybe this wasn't such a good idea, coming up here again, I—" She fairly jumped at the loud crack that shook the heavens and the house. Her eyes widened. "What was that?"

He'd instinctively placed his hand on her shoulder. The way she stiffened had him dropping it immediately. "Thunder." Morgan glanced toward the living room. "From the looks of it, your dog isn't too keen on that, either."

Traci turned to look behind her. From where

she stood she could see Jeremiah slipping under the rug he'd just been lying on. Argument forgotten, Traci hurried over to the dog.

"Poor baby." She sank down on her knees beside the animal. "It's all right, Jeremiah, just noise. Nothing else."

She wasn't aware that Morgan was right behind her until he spoke. "You'd think he'd be used to noise, being your dog. You still talk to anything with ears?"

It didn't sound like an insult, so she smiled. "Yeah."

Morgan folded his legs under him as he sat down on the floor beside her. "Here." He handed her a fresh mug of coffee. "Sorry, out of sugar."

Traci took it from him. "I'll just dip my finger in."

"That should spice it up," he commented dryly.

Sipping, Traci stroked the animal's fur slowly, knowing the repetitive action would soothe him. The coffee didn't taste half-bad, even without sugar.

She raised her eyes to his. "Thanks."

Morgan shrugged. "No sense in throwing out a good pot of coffee."

Had he always had this core of shyness? she wondered. "Very prudent. Did you get economical after your father lost all that money?"

"I had to. Suddenly things I always thought I couldn't live without were expendable." It had made him take stock of what was really important to him.

She cocked her head, her fingers still tangled in Jeremiah's fur. "Like Cynthia?"

"Yeah."

She saw something flicker in his eyes. For once, she didn't want to return to old ground. "Sorry, low blow."

He lifted a shoulder and let it drop carelessly, unfazed. "I'm used to it with you."

"Very gracious of you." She hesitated. For a moment she actually wanted to tell him about Rory. She hadn't the faintest idea why.

Thunder rolled again. Jeremiah emitted a low moan. Time to get things moving. "I'd better take a walk out back before the storm hits."

He rose to his feet. "That might not be such a bad idea," he agreed. "This storm might not come for hours," he mused, "but then again—"

"It might be here in five minutes," she concluded. In which case, she'd better get on the road. She wanted to get back to the city before any storm of consequence hit.

Morgan took her hand in his and pulled her to her feet. Her body slid against his, igniting a very pleasant sensation.

"You know," she murmured, "if it wasn't you, I would have said that was a choreographed move."

"And if it was anyone but you," he countered, "I would have said you went along with it willingly."

"Good thing we know each other."

"Good thing," he echoed, following her out the back door.

But he couldn't help wondering if they did.

4

Traci pulled the sleeves of her sweater down to cover her arms, hunching her shoulders slightly against the wind. The incline from the house to the dock below felt steeper than she remembered. She took smaller steps. Age had taken away some of her bravado and made her more careful. So had the fear of falling in front of Morgan and making a fool of herself.

The weather didn't help. It was more suited for a homecoming to a dark, gloomy castle on a lonely cliff than a warm summerhouse nestled beside a lake.

It had been a long time since anything had been tied here, she mused as she looked along the dock. Morgan's father had owned a small motorboat, but she had favored the kayak he'd left for her and Morgan to use. There had been room for two, but she usually got to it first and was on the lake before Morgan was up. They fought about the kayak a lot.

And once, she remembered, sitting down on the edge of the dock, the kayak had been more than just the source of conflict. It had caused Morgan to be a hero. He'd saved her from an ignoble, watery end. The kayak had capsized, something she'd been completely convinced that it couldn't do, and she hadn't been able to right it, or get out. Her feet had somehow gotten stuck inside. Morgan had been the only one on the dock at the time. She'd abandoned him there. He'd seen the kayak go over and he'd jumped in, swimming out to her rescue.

Morgan hadn't let her forget about that one for a long time.

Traci braced her hands on either side of her. The dock felt rough to the touch. Needed work, she mused. The whole house did, really. But it was well worth the effort in her opinion. She hated to think of it as belonging to someone else.

Traci lifted her chin, letting the wind rake spiky, ghostly fingers over her face. Her hair was whipping around her head like curly blond snakes. She looked, Morgan thought, like an illustration for unharnessed mischief.

Or a temptress.

"It's a lot more beautiful than I remember." She nodded toward the lake. On the other side was a pristine, three-story white house. It appeared closer to her than she recalled. Her mouth curved. "And maybe a little smaller."

There was something almost soft about her, Morgan noted. A dimension she probably wanted to keep under wraps.

"And darker." Rain was only minutes away, if that long.

"That, too." She looked up at the angry sky. It was as if a huge, dark comforter was being slipped over them. "It looks like it's going to be a mean one."

He laughed shortly to himself. "Reminds me a little of you."

The comment caught her by surprise. "I was never mean." Morgan arched a brow at the protest. "All right," she relented slightly. She could see how he might have misinterpreted her actions over the years. "But not *mean*-mean."

Leave it to Traci to be obscure about something so straightforward and simple. "That terminology might fit right into a long-running children's program where the guy is forever changing his shoes to sneakers and back again, but I'm not sure I follow the distinction here.''

Traci blew out a breath. It was lost in the wind. ''I was just being a kid—''

He shook his head at her explanation. ''Not like any kid I ever knew.''

It was getting really chilly and she shivered. Morgan curbed the urge to put his arm around her. She'd probably bite it off, just like a fox gnawing off its own foot to be free of a trap.

Traci squared her shoulders. The wind ran right up her back. ''I'll take that as a compliment.''

He put a pin to her bubble. ''It wasn't intended as one.''

''Never mind.'' She sniffed, hiding her grin. ''Too late.''

Funny how he was amused by the very thing that would have sent him up a wall a decade ago. ''With you, it was too late from the first moment.''

''If you mean you were a dead duck from the minute our parents introduced us, you were smarter back then than I gave you credit for.''

He opened his mouth to answer, then thought better of it. It was futile to battle it out verbally with her. Morgan knew by experience that one way or another, Traci would always come out on top. It was the warrior instinct in her.

The description made him smile.

''What?''

He shook his head. ''Never mind.''

Jeremiah, safely ensconced in the house, howled his displeasure about being left behind. Morgan looked behind him and saw the dog through the screen door. Jeremiah was hardly more than a dark shadow. A dark shadow that was trying to paw through the mesh and get out, he noted.

"Where did you ever find him?" As Traci began to answer, Morgan stopped her. "No, let me guess. He's a stray."

Jeremiah didn't look like a mutt that had lived on the street. "How did you know?"

That was easy. Morgan's short laugh was swallowed up by the wind. "You're the type to take in strays."

Something about the set of his mouth as he said that alerted her. "Is this leading up to another crack about Daniel?"

"Hardly." *Touchy, touchy.* He had to have struck a nerve earlier, Morgan thought. Maybe she really was having strong doubts about marrying this dentist of hers, just as he'd suggested.

He looked up at the sky and thought about getting back. But there was something oddly nice about sitting out here with her. He didn't know which was more invigorating, Traci or the wind. "A successful dentist who has two practices in New York City can't be considered a stray by any stretch of the imagination."

She turned toward him, pulling her legs up against her body for warmth and wrapping her arms around them. "How do you know so much about him?'' Before he could say anything, she had her answer. "My mother, right?''

He nodded, completing the thought. "Your mother relates information to my mother who, in turn, feels honor bound to pass it on to me, as if I would be missing something if I didn't know.'' The look on his face told Traci what he thought of *that* idea. "I think she hopes that our sense of competition will have me running to the nearest altar.''

Traci rocked back, studying him. A smile played on her lips. "Little good that'll do you alone.''

"She was hoping I'd bring someone with me,'' he said dryly.

"So, why don't you?'' She would have expected someone like Morgan to have already been married five years and working on his second child. "You're young, reasonably attractive,'' she paused, catching her tongue between her teeth, "and some women even like lawyers—''

He looked away. The water was getting choppier on the lake, like a bathtub where a child was conducting a battle with toy ships. It was going to be a big one when it hit, he thought.

"Thanks for the crumbs, but the truth is that I haven't found anyone.''

How hard could that be? She stared at him incredulously. "My God, Morgan, you found Cynthia. Anyone else could only be a step up.''

"Maybe.'' He shrugged. "But I've been too busy to step anywhere—up or down.''

His words stirred a memory. "That was always your excuse."

He looked at her, surprised.

"If you hadn't hidden behind your schoolwork, you wouldn't have been such ripe prey for someone like Cynthia."

Morgan didn't see the connection, but then, he didn't have Traci's convoluted way of thinking, either. "What's that supposed to mean?"

For a supposedly smart man, Morgan could be very dumb sometimes. Traci recited the answer in a singsong voice, as if she was trying to get the concept across to a child. "You lacked experience and were an easy target for a shark."

He had a strange, bemused expression on his face.

"What's the matter?"

He leaned closer so his words weren't blown away before they reached her. "I just had a sudden vision of this turning up in your strip." The look in her eyes didn't lay his suspicions to rest. "It won't, will it?"

She looked at Morgan innocently. Now that he mentioned it...

"No, why should it? This is your life, remember? Not mine."

That didn't assure him. She sounded much too innocent. "Yes, but somehow the edges have gotten blurred since I've been talking to you about it." The Traci in the strip had a best friend named Velma with whom she dissected practically everything. He could just see himself being dissected by the two.

Traci raised her hand as if making a solemn promise. Mentally, she crossed her fingers. All was fair in love, war and comic strips.

"Don't worry, I'll leave you out of it. Although the thought of drawing a shark with Cynthia's face does have its appeal."

He could see where it might for her, and if he were being completely honest, the thought appealed to him, as well. With one stipulation.

"Well, if she does turn up, I'd appreciate it if you draw her nibbling away at someone else." The last thing in the world he wanted was to open the morning paper and look at a caricature of himself mooning at a sharklike Cynthia.

"Rory," Traci muttered to herself. Someone like Cynthia should have feasted on someone like Rory. They deserved each other.

"Who?"

Traci looked at him in surprise. She hadn't realized that she'd said the name out loud. "Hmm?"

Morgan moved closer to her. He had no desire to shout. "You said a name."

Funny, how with all this wind she could still smell his cologne. She had no idea what it was, only that she liked it. Maybe a tad too much.

"No, I didn't," she protested staunchly.

He knew she had. "Roy?" he guessed. It had sounded something like that.

She'd be damned if she was going to play twenty questions about her past. She might want him to bare his soul, but hers was staying right where it was, hidden. No one else knew about Rory and it was going to stay that way. She had better things to do than publicize her own stupidity. It was far more entertaining to tease Morgan about his.

Pity filled her eyes. "Approaching thirty and losing your hearing already. What a shame."

He was about to say something about the wind being responsible when a large splotch of rain hit Traci directly in the face. Even larger drops followed in rapid succession, falling harder and faster.

Morgan rose to his feet at the same time she jumped to hers. "Yikes," she cried. "These drops are as big as swimming pools."

Without thinking, Morgan grabbed her hand and they ran up the hill toward the house.

"'Yikes'?" he echoed. "Who the hell says yikes these days? You've been watching too many cartoons."

"Never too many." She laughed as they made it through the back door. And just in time. Suddenly, sheets of rain began falling.

Jeremiah, agitated and distressed by the weather, almost managed to knock Morgan down as they hurried in. Morgan grabbed for the doorjamb and shifted out of the way just in time.

Running a hand through his hair to shake off the rain, Morgan glared at the dog. "Can't you train this animal?"

She managed to maintain a straight face for almost a minute. "Not a problem. Jeremiah," she said, looking sternly at the dog. "Knock him down. See?" Traci turned a sunny smile on Morgan. "He almost did it."

When was he ever going to learn? "Do you ever get serious?"

Traci pushed her hair out of her face in the careless manner of a woman who was content with her looks in any situation.

"Not if I can help it. It doesn't pay. Too depressing."

She'd always been just a little too crazy for his tastes. "You know, there is a happy medium between Kafka and Jocko the Clown."

"Tell me when you find it." She looked down and saw that there was a small puddle forming on the floor where she stood. She'd gotten wetter than she thought in that short run. "You have any more towels around here, or do I just stand dripping on your floor?"

"Sorry, this is all I have. I wasn't expecting a storm." His eyes washed over her as he passed her the lone towel. "Although, maybe I should have been."

She fluttered her eyes at him the way she'd done when she'd imitated Cynthia. "You say the sweetest things." Traci rubbed the towel through her hair quickly, then offered it back to him.

Morgan took it, vaguely aware that her scent was clinging to it. It became more potent when he brought the towel closer. Disturbed, he dropped it on the back of his chair.

Something moved through him, restless and unsettled when he looked at her.

He had to be crazy to be having these feelings about her. She was just as competitive, just as irritating, as ever. And she was about to be engaged. Any way he looked at it, the package was not inviting.

Or wasn't supposed to be.

Avoiding her eyes, Morgan crossed to the window. "Not exactly the greatest weather for a reunion." The trees directly outside the window were bending to and fro, like stately dancers doing stretching exercises before their performance. "You'd think the weather bureau could be right once in a while."

Traci stroked Jeremiah's head, then moved beside Morgan. It was really beginning to look foul out there. Her first weekend off in months and it had to turn into this.

She shrugged philosophically. "What? And spoil a perfect record? Not hardly. Think it's easy always being wrong?" she quipped.

He turned to look at her. She was back on the floor, stroking that wimp of a dog of hers. "I don't know. Is it?"

"Oh, low blow." She grinned, and somehow the storm stepped back a few feet away from them. "I like that. You're beginning to show promise."

The look in her eyes warmed him.

The crack of thunder made Traci jump back to her feet. "I think it's time to take this show on the road before there isn't a road to take it on." But even as she said it, Traci found herself not wanting to leave just yet. As if, once she walked out the door, she'd be closing a chapter of her life forever.

It was a silly thought, but she couldn't shake it.

"You might be right," Morgan agreed and then grinned at her. "I guess there has to be a first time for everything."

"Just because I said I liked that low blow doesn't mean you should get carried away. A little sarcasm is a good thing, but there is such a thing as overkill."

"You ought to know," he murmured. There was humor in her eyes and he was drawn to it.

Every inclination directed her toward the door and the road beyond. She was right in wanting to leave before the road became impassable. And yet something—she wasn't sure just what—was telling her to linger a little longer. Linger despite common sense and a whining dog to the contrary.

She supposed there was no harm in giving in for a couple more minutes. Traci pretended to look around for her purse, stalling.

"You never told me—why are your parents selling the house now?"

She would have thought that was something they would have done during that low period they'd experienced, not now, when, according to her mother, everything was going so well for them. Jim Brigham's company had not only re-gained its former ground but grown beyond it.

Morgan paused, looking for the right words to frame his answer. "They want to be free to travel around in, to put it my mother's way, 'the sunset of their years.'" He shrugged, looking around as if he hadn't done so a dozen times already before she'd arrived. "My guess is that the house was beginning to need too many things—"

"Like good storm windows?" There was a def-inite chill in the air that seemed to be coming from outside despite the fact that everything ap-peared to be locked up tight.

He'd noticed the draft earlier; he nodded. "And other things." He was warming to his explana-tion. "They were beginning to think of it as a burden, so they asked me to sell it for them."

She could guess at the practical reasons behind it, but she wasn't all that crazy about practicality. No matter how much Daniel swore by it, she thought suddenly. The unexpected thought un-nerved her.

"Seems a shame to let it go."

He studied her closely. "Why? It's falling apart."

She sniffed her contempt of his view. "You *would* only see that."

Morgan set his jaw hard and folded his arms before him. "What do you see?"

Her expression softened as if she were looking beyond the walls. "Memories."

Habit as ingrained as breathing had him challenging her. "I don't need a building to see that. Memories are in your head and your heart and, occasionally, in an album."

Her eyes widened as she looked at him. "Why, Morgan, that's positively poetic."

Morgan knew better than to take her comment at face value. He waited for a punch line. She wasn't about to disappoint him.

"Limited," she added airily, "but poetic."

He knew he could count on Traci. "Okay, I'll bite. Why limited?"

She glanced toward the fireplace in the living room and wished for a fire. It only reminded her that she really should be leaving.

"Because if we followed your way of thinking, no one would have ever bothered with preserving historic landmarks."

He couldn't help laughing at the comparison. "This house is hardly a historic landmark."

The man was hopeless. "No, not to the world. But to those of us who spent a lot of time here..." She stopped and looked at him. "You don't feel anything, do you?"

"Confused," he volunteered. "Does that count?"

Traci laughed as she hit his chest playfully with the flat of her hand. "No, that doesn't—"

The next thing she knew, Jeremiah was up and growling at Morgan as fiercely as if he'd just uncovered an entire battalion of enemy soldiers—or cats.

Traci made a grab for the dog's collar a second

before he reared at Morgan. Teeth snapped with a menacing finality.

Morgan took a step back uneasily. "What's his problem?"

"I guess Jeremiah thought we were fighting and he was coming to my rescue."

Those teeth really did look large close up. And lethal. So much for thinking the dog a wimp. "Better tether him if you and Daniel ever argue."

Traci stroked Jeremiah until the dog calmed down again. With a tentative yawn, he lay down at her feet. "We don't argue."

Morgan laughed out loud and Traci looked at him accusingly.

"Oh, come on, Traci. This is me. I know you. You'd argue with God."

She stuck by her statement. It was the truth. "Daniel and I don't argue."

As she said them, her own words made her think. Why *didn't* they argue? Normal people argued. She more than most, although she wasn't about to admit that point to Morgan.

He looked at her closely. "You're really serious." True concern nudged him on. And maybe just a little bit of hope. "Traci, I was only kidding earlier, but maybe you should really think about this. He obviously can't be the one for you. You need passion in your life, zest. The kind of man who can make you argue. A man who can periodically take you and shake you up—and you him."

Realizing he was saying a hell of a lot more

than he intended to, Morgan abruptly stopped talking.

He wasn't telling her anything she hadn't thought herself, in the wee hours of the morning when the world was its blackest and doubts loomed their largest. The fact that she agreed, however, wouldn't have stopped her from taking umbrage at his words.

What stopped her was the look in Morgan's eyes. He wasn't baiting her, wasn't trying to arouse her ire. He was serious.

As if he cared.

The way she had cared when she had thought of Morgan throwing away his life on someone like Cynthia. It gave her pause and momentarily took away her tongue.

When she found it, she spoke quietly. "He's a good man, Morgan."

Morgan wasn't quite sure exactly how he had gotten in so close to her, he only knew that, somehow, they were standing almost toe-to-toe and the distance was rapidly shrinking, even though neither one of them was moving a muscle.

"So's the pope. You're not marrying him."

A half smile curved her full mouth. "No, he didn't ask."

Her answer told him more than she realized. "So, you are marrying Daniel?"

She thought that one over carefully. Slowly, she nodded. "I think so."

Morgan resisted believing her. Because he didn't think that in her heart she believed herself.

"That doesn't sound like the Traci I know. The one who runs headlong into things without thinking."

No, it didn't. She forced a smile to her lips. "Maybe I've grown up."

He remained unconvinced. "I don't think so. Not you. Not like this."

She lifted her chin, suddenly feeling very uneasy, as if the ground beneath her feet were liquefying. But that was impossible. That happened only during an earthquake, and they didn't get earthquakes out here.

Only storms.

Like the one swirling around her now.

"What would you know about it?" she challenged, digging for some of her customary bravado. "You haven't seen me in, what, eight years?"

"Nine," he corrected softly.

Very lightly, he feathered his fingers along her face. He couldn't seem to help himself. Nor could he help this feeling that was taking hold of him against his will.

It *was* against his will, wasn't it?

"And I know." He smiled into her eyes, quieting her protest, as if anything earthly actually could. "I read your strip."

"I already told you, Morgan. All that's exaggerated." The words were supposed to be shouted. But they merely dripped from her lips like a faucet that wasn't quite turned off.

"Yes, I know." His face, his lips, drew closer. "But so are you."

Something was twisting inside her stomach. "Morgan?" she whispered.

"Hmm?" She seemed to be all around him, invading his senses like a virus.

She ran the tip of her tongue over her parched lips. "You're standing too close."

He cupped her cheek. "No, I'm not. I can't kiss you from across the room."

"Oh." Slowly, she nodded her head, as if in a trance. And maybe, just maybe, she was in one. Otherwise, she'd be running for her life. Because what she was feeling was scaring her. "Good reason." Her throat had never felt so dry in her whole life. As dry as the world outside the window was wet.

And then his lips touched hers and the world outside might as well have existed on another planet.

Because she certainly did.

WELL, AT LEAST IT MAKES A GOOD NIGHT-LIGHT.

5

She heard them.

She actually heard them. Bells. Banjos. And maybe even a sousaphone thrown in for good measure. They were all there, an entire symphony full of them. Along with music she couldn't place and a rush of fire that threatened to consume everything in its path.

Her, first of all.

She'd seen the kiss coming. But what she hadn't foreseen was what could come after. Nothing could have prepared her for that.

Caught completely off guard, Traci had no defenses against the feeling that swept over her with the speed of a flame eating its way up a narrow line of gunpowder. And because her head was spinning around like a carousel at warp speed, she had no desire to offer any, either.

Breathless, intoxicated, Traci allowed herself to be taken away by the feeling. To savor it, to revel in it. Most of all, to be awed by it.

It was almost like when Rory kissed her. Almost but not quite.

This was different.

Better.

Her fingers tightened on Morgan's shoulders as she rose on her toes to surrender completely to the sensation. It was absolutely incredible.

Traci?

Her name throbbed in Morgan's mind as bewildering, demanding sensations throbbed in other parts of his body.

This was *Traci?*

How a woman who had been as irritating as scratchy long winter underwear for more than a decade of his life, who was damn irritating *now,* could possibly inspire this rush he was feeling—

this bone melting, mind numbing reaction that made him want to plunge himself into the kiss, into her, and never come up for air—was completely beyond him.

He couldn't begin to fathom it.

Traci?

Naw, couldn't be.

And yet, here she was, in his arms, sealed to his mouth, sucking out life forces from him with a speed that had Morgan reeling. And wanting more. A hell of a lot more.

The very thought that he wanted to make love with her sobered him even as it threatened to send him over the edge.

Shaken, dazed and more confused than he'd possibly ever been in his life, Morgan drew away from her. But as if some part of him refused to let go, he found himself still holding on to her arms.

Morgan's eyes narrowed as he studied her face. Yes, it was Traci. No doubt about it. What was in doubt, though, was his sanity. So much the more because part of him, against all odds, had suspected this all along.

Traci swallowed. It didn't help. Her throat felt dry, scratchy. She was aware of everything around her. She could have even sworn that she could feel her hair growing.

"Were you trying to prove a point?" The question came out in a low whisper. Anything louder and she knew her voice would crack. Or even give out completely. And when had it gotten so damn hot in here? She blew out a breath. Her bangs fluttered against her damp forehead.

Pulses throughout Morgan's body scrambled to reclaim positions. He cleared his throat. "I don't know, was I?"

If he had been, it was completely lost on him. As were his bearings and, just possibly, his name, rank and serial number.

Very slowly, the world came back into focus for Traci. This was ridiculous. She couldn't be having this kind of a reaction to Morgan. Not *Morgan*. They were friendly enemies, competitors, maybe even fond of each other, but nothing more.

But if that was true, how the hell had he managed to evoke this wild, erotic tune that was even now still ricocheting in her brain?

"What's the matter?" he asked. She had an odd expression on her face. Did she feel as disoriented as he did? It would help if she did. Not a hell of a whole lot, but some.

Traci slowly shook her head before answering, trying to buy herself a little more time.

"Nothing," she mumbled. Then her eyes looked up at him, wide with wonder. She had to say it. "You never kissed me before."

He would have, he thought, if he'd known that kissing her could pack such a wallop. But admitting it would put him at a disadvantage. "It never came up."

She could only stare at him incredulously, willing her knees back among the functioning. "And it did now?"

He had to make light of it. If he didn't, she'd see right through him—down to the shaken mess that was passing as his soul at the moment.

"We were standing close, your lips were there." He shrugged, at a loss as to where to go from here. "I don't know, maybe I was struck temporarily insane."

It seemed as good an explanation as any, at least to him. Why else would he have kissed her? It wasn't as if he was actually attracted to her. Sure, she was pretty, gorgeous, even, in the right light, but he *knew* her. Knew what she was like. How could he be attracted to a woman who had once put red ants into his sandwich?

And yet, hadn't he, in some small, imperceptible way, been attracted to her all along? Hadn't he wondered, in the back of his mind, what it would be like to kiss her?

Well, now he knew. And it blew out all the stops.

There was something more there, Traci thought. She could see it in his face. Or maybe she was just hoping there was more—to placate herself and her still erratically fluttering pulse.

"Is that your best defense, Counselor?"

"That's my best explanation," he clarified. And then, because he believed in telling the truth, or at least some measure of it, he relented. "It's either that, or call you a witch."

She didn't knew whether to be annoyed or amused. "So this is my fault now, is it?"

"Not so much a fault as—" He stopped as a thought struck him. "Do you kiss Donald this way?"

"Daniel," Traci corrected. Donald was the name of her cartoon suitor. *Traci's* cartoon suitor, she amended, annoyed at herself for the slip. Annoyance shifted to a more likely target. "And that's none of your business."

Maybe, but he thought it was. And he did have a point to make. "Okay, but if you do kiss him like that, and he's still as bland as he sounds, I'd check the man for a pulse—or, barring that, antennae."

Now he had really lost her. "What?"

Morgan hated admitting any more than he already had, but he supposed he had to. "Nothing human could have withstood that and not felt his socks getting short-circuited."

Indignation and confusion slowly slipped away, replaced with a glimmer of a satisfied smile. So he *had* felt something. Hopefully, more than she had, although she wasn't certain how that was humanly possible. "Is that a compliment?"

She looked like a cat that had fallen headfirst into a vat of cream. He refused to give her an ounce more. "That's an observation."

She knew it was more than that, but for both their sakes she played along and nodded. A fresh crack of thunder and Jeremiah's accompanying wail only served as a distant backdrop to the scenario going on before her. Her mouth still felt as if it was throbbing. And the rest of her was vibrating like a tuning fork.

Traci knew she had to leave. Now, before something unforeseeable happened. Something she would undoubtedly live to regret.

She nodded again, dumbly, like a windup toy with one trick. That Morgan had managed to disorient her to this extent really annoyed her. "I guess you're not so bad yourself."

The cast-off comment had him smiling. If she admitted to smoke, there most certainly was fire. "Gosh, can you spare that?"

Traci blew out a breath. It was still far too shaky for her liking. "Just barely. Well, like I said, I'd better be going."

She was backing up, away from Morgan. Away from what she'd just experienced, even though a very large part of her wanted to move forward, to explore this new, uncharted region a little more.

Wanted to feel a little more.

To feel more. Traci almost mocked herself. She'd been that route and knew the danger that laid therein. All sensation, no substance.

But that had been Rory and this...

This was Morgan, for heaven's sake. She's seen him naked, albeit years ago, but still, there was no mystery here—except, maybe, that she would have never dreamed in a million years...

Nope, never.

She groped for her purse. Time for Cinderella to rush home while she still had a pumpkin to work with. Traci clapped her hands and Jeremiah came at her call. She picked up his leash, wrapping it firmly around her hand. If nothing else, it served as insulation against Morgan.

Only then did she look at him again. "It's been an experience, Morgan. One we'll have to do again—in about another nine or ten years. But right now, I have a storm to beat." She found she had to force cheeriness into her voice.

He didn't want her leaving and he definitely didn't like the idea of her leaving in this kind of weather. It was particularly nasty outside. "Ordinarily, I'd say my money was on you when it came to beating anything." He glanced out the window. "But it looks pretty bad out there, Traci."

For some reason, she found the serious note in his voice unsettling. She liked it better when they were sparring. She felt equipped to handle that, not this shaky vulnerability he'd managed to uncover.

"Don't worry, I'll be fine." *As soon as my double vision goes away,* she thought, giving her head one more shake.

She glanced at Morgan over her shoulder as she opened the door. *It had to have been a fluke.* Maybe she was coming down with something. That had to be it. Otherwise, she'd have to think that she and Morgan...

No, she didn't have to think that. Not ever. Besides, it was too late for something like that. She had her commitment before her and it was to Daniel.

"I'll see you around," she told him, raising her voice above the wind. Traci gave the leash a slight tug. "Let's go, Jeremiah."

The dog resisted crossing the threshold. He barked twice at the brooding, darkened sky.

Morgan wondered what sort of perverse psychology he could use on Traci to make her stay. Nothing came to mind and he knew that asking her to wait out the storm would never work.

He nodded toward her pet. "He has more sense than you do."

Morgan was standing way too close again, she thought. Driving in the storm would be a comfort by comparison. At least that didn't involve scrambling pulses and confused thoughts.

"Lovely parting shot, Morgan," she quipped. "You should put them all in a book and give them out as gifts for Christmas. Well, see you." Her voice was way too high, but nerves were causing that.

Thousands of little nerves, scattered throughout her body like ants whose hill had just been demolished by an overeager anteater.

Traci almost fled to her car.

She should have parked closer, she thought, annoyed with herself. She should have also left earlier—for a lot of reasons. But that was a moot point now.

The wind lashed at her hair, whipping it around her head and reducing it to a soggy, springy mass of curls within seconds. Muttering under her breath, Traci opened the car door and herded Jeremiah in, then rounded the hood and got in on the driver's side. She jammed the key into the ignition, pushing wet bangs out of her eyes.

She held her breath as she drove. The downpour was pretty intense, but it was too late to turn back. She refused to return with her tail between her legs because of the storm. Not when she would bet her soul that Morgan was standing in the doorway, waiting for her to come back. Waiting to smugly say, "I told you so."

Or worse yet, to kiss her again and watch the reaction on her face.

What had happened back there, anyway? Why the sudden combustion? It was as if something had just been lying in wait all these years, lying in wait for the right moment.

This wasn't getting her anywhere.

A bolt of lightning creased the sky like a crooked javelin hurled by an angry Norse god. It temporarily threw the world into daylight and then back into numbing darkness again.

Jeremiah was not happy about it.

"Hush," she chided. "We'll be home in time to watch reruns of 'Lassie.' They have to be playing on some channel." The thought of curling up on her sofa, basking in the warm glow cast from the television set, comforted her.

It was a hell of a lot more comforting than attempting to drive through the English Channel, which was what this was beginning to feel like, she thought. She pressed her lips together, concentrating.

Visibility went from poor to almost nonexistent in an alarming few minutes, even though the windshield wipers were doing double time. They no sooner pushed the rain aside than another deluge fell to take up the space, completely blotting out her view of the road. And no matter what she did with the heater and the defrost switches, her windows insisted on fogging up. The situation was almost impossible.

Desperate, Traci rolled down the window on the driver's side, cracking the other for balance. Rain came into the car, lashing at her face. But at least she could see. What there was to see.

Craning her neck, Traci peered through the open window. She squinted, trying to make out the road that rain and encroaching darkness were bent on obscuring.

Holding her breath, Traci drove slower than she'd ever driven in her life. The wind continued to pick up, howling. Jeremiah joined in the competition.

It got on her nerves. "I hope you don't intend to do that all the way home. I'm fresh out of aspirin." And patience, she added silently.

She should have remained in the house with Morgan, she told herself. She realized that her jaw was clenched, as clenched as her fingers were on the steering wheel. Focusing, she tried to ease up on both. But the tension in her shoulders persisted.

And there was something more. The wind had initially masked it, but now the sound grew louder. Water. Rushing water. It took her a second to make the connection. The gully beneath the bridge had filled with water. That meant she had to be getting close to it.

Damn it, where was the bridge? Why couldn't she see it? It had to be here somewhere.

Traci craned her neck farther, searching for the small wooden structure. Crossing it earlier, she'd thought that time had made the bridge almost rickety. Not that it had ever been all that strong to begin with. And in this weather it would have to be—

Gone.

Fear seemed to manually force her heart into her throat where it remained, stuck, as Traci realized that she was now directly over where the bridge should have been.

And there was nothing there.

The edges of her front tires were touching nothing. The headache that had been threatening to engulf her ever since she left the house made an appearance, full bodied and strong. It pounded over her temples and forehead like a scorned, irate lover as Traci frantically threw the car into reverse, trying to keep the car from plunging straight into the gully.

She overcompensated, turning the steering wheel too far to the left, and the car went speeding backward, making contact with a tree.

Shrieking, Traci slammed on her brakes, but it

was after the fact. The collision was already in motion. Metal against wood.

It felt as if something vital had been jarred loose in her body as she hit her forehead against the steering wheel. The last thing she heard was Jeremiah's mournful cry.

And then there was an inky blackness dropping over her, too heavy to resist.

Her eyelids weighed a ton. Each one. It took her several vain attempts to pry open her eyes. Each time she tried, she found she couldn't lift them. It was as if they were nailed down.

Traci thought she heard a voice. Someone was talking to her, but she couldn't place who it was or what was being said. And there were shadows moving, drifting here and there. Some belonged to the voice. Others didn't.

Each time she was sure she'd opened her eyes and looked, she discovered that she hadn't.

It was frustrating as hell.

Traci moaned, trying to turn, to sit up, confident that if she did, her eyes would open.

She began to make things out more clearly. There were hands holding her down. Gentle hands. Strong hands. She struggled against them and lost that fight, too. There seemed to be no energy flowing through her. Nothing. No blood.

Blood.

Jeremiah.

Oh, God, she'd killed Jeremiah. She'd heard his pitiful moan just before she—what?

Where was she? Traci twisted again, but the same two hands were holding her down. They were pressing on her arms. She fought, struggled, tried to speak, and still her eyes refused to budge.

Was it a dream? Was she dead?

It was a lot drier where she was.

Heaven?

In the distance somewhere, she heard the crackle of something. Fire?

Was she in hell? She groaned in fear.

"Damn it, even when you're unconscious, you're a problem."

Morgan, that was Morgan's voice. Was he dead, too? No, she'd left him in the house. Him and his lips.

With supreme effort, Traci concentrated on the sound of his voice, on surfacing out of this cottony netherworld she was trapped in.

Inch by inch, she made it to the top. Her eyes finally flew open and focused on Morgan. He was looming over her, almost larger than life. And he was holding her down. Touching her. Never mind that it was only her arms. She could feel it all along her body.

This had to stop.

"Get your hands off me," she breathed.

Grasping at indignation and hoping it would give her the shot of adrenaline she needed, Traci bolted upright. A second later, she became one with the pain that rushed up to greet her. Her head felt like an egg that had been cracked open against the side of a pan.

Instinctively, her hand went to her head. There was a bandage there.

"What the—?"

Morgan grabbed her wrist and firmly held on to it. "Leave that alone," he ordered. "You hit your head on the steering wheel and cut your forehead." When he saw that she was actually going to listen to him, he released her wrist. "Although I didn't think anything as hard as that could be cut by anything less than the sharp edge of a diamond."

Everything felt as if it were submerged in her mind, mired in thick chicken soup. She looked around. She was back in the house. On the sofa. Before the fireplace. But that was impossible.

"How did I get here?"

The color was returning to her cheeks. That was a good sign. She'd given him one hell of a scare back there. When he had found her slumped over the steering wheel, he'd thought she was dead. It had taken him a moment to quell and manage the panic that had shot through him. "I brought you back here."

She drew her brows together and found that it hurt. "You?"

He lifted a shoulder and then let it drop carelessly. "Sir Lancelot was busy."

It still didn't make any sense to her. She'd left him in the house. How could he have known she was in an accident? And why was he all wet?

"Why—? How—?"

Since neither one of them was going anywhere,

Morgan sat down on the edge of the sofa beside her.

"The 'why' is because I didn't think leaving you out in the rain was such a good idea. And the 'how' is that I carried you." His mouth curved. Now that she was conscious, he could allow himself that luxury. "You weigh less than I thought."

Traci tried to assimilate what he was telling her, feeding it into her brain above the pounding pain. She held her head, afraid that if she didn't, it would fall off.

"But I left you in here," she began, hoping that saying the words aloud would somehow help her make sense out of her scattered thoughts. It didn't. She couldn't seem to get them in order.

Watching her car disappear into the rain had given him a very uneasy feeling. Morgan had waited five minutes, maybe six, before finally getting into his own car and following her. He'd arrived just in time to watch her car travel backward into the tree. Racing from his car to hers had been the longest and worst minute of his life.

"I'm ambulatory in case you haven't noticed." He might as well tell her the whole truth. "I was worried and decided to go out looking for you. Lucky thing for you I did. We're marooned out here, at least for the duration of the storm. My distributor cap decided to play dead just as I got to the lovely mess that used to be your car."

The reason for the car's sudden shuddering and then sputtering halt had registered in his mind only after the fact. Nothing had registered at the time except that her car was crashing right before his eyes. And that she was in it.

Traci winced as the memory returned. "My car—it's bad?"

"Only if you want to drive it. As an accordion it still has possibilities." He became serious. It could have very well gone a different way. "You're damn lucky to be alive."

She was almost afraid to ask. But she had to know. "Jeremiah—?"

He'd dragged the dumb mutt along with him in his wake. It hadn't been easy but he wasn't about to abandon the mangy animal in the storm.

"Smells like hell wet," he informed her gently. "Can't you smell him?"

She took a deep breath and then visibly calmed down. "Now I can." Her eyes turned to his and she mustered a smile, despite the pain that was splitting her head in half. "Thanks."

Morgan made light of her gratitude. Accepting it was more difficult than he thought.

"Don't mention it. It was selfish, anyway." He saw her brows draw together. "Your mother would have killed me if I let anything happen to you."

"Can't have that happening," she murmured. She was vaguely aware that Jeremiah had moved closer to her. Hand dangling over the side of the sofa, Traci managed to lightly run her fingers over his wet coat. It was a comforting gesture.

Almost as comforting as having Morgan sitting beside her.

6

If someone had ever attempted to tell him that Traci had a vulnerable side, Morgan would have laughed him out of the room. But there was no other word that could describe the way she looked lying there on the sofa, her eyes half-closed, the bandage taped to her forehead. He had this overwhelming urge to take care of her. An urge he knew would irritate her if she suspected it.

He'd felt this way about her only once before, he remembered. The time he'd saved her when she was drowning. But all that had happened so fast, he hadn't had time to dwell on it.

He did now.

A strange, bittersweet feeling drifted through him. He never realized how frail she looked. Morgan took Traci's hand between his. It felt small and cold. "How do you feel?"

Much too much. It was as if something was opening inside of her. Opening like a flower to the sun after a long rainy period. Opening and being drawn to Morgan. It had to be the result of the trauma to her head, she thought. There was no other explanation for it. She wasn't going to let there be another explanation for it.

"I'm all right," she murmured. "A little woozy, but under the circumstances, I guess that's allowed."

She felt a great deal more than that, but with luck, it would pass. Her mother liked to brag that the women in the Richardson family were made of stern, pioneer stock. Right now, she felt like a pioneer woman a cow had stepped on.

He wasn't quite certain he believed her protest. "I tried to call for an ambulance, but the phone isn't working. The storm must have knocked out the lines."

All this and heaven, too. "I don't need an ambulance,'' Traci said with the first ounce of feeling he'd heard since she'd opened her eyes. It made him feel a little better about her condition. ''I just have to lie here for a few minutes, that's all.''

He nodded. Right now, that seemed to be the only thing they could do, anyway. Morgan looked down at her. The sofa was turning dark from the water it was leeching from her clothes.

''You're going to have to get out of those wet things.'' Advice he should follow himself, he thought. His own were sticking to him and felt clammy along his body.

''You know, if it was anyone but you saying this, I would have said that you had an ulterior motive.''

The idea had already crossed his mind—more than once—but now wasn't the time to tell her. Probably never was more like it.

''Well, it is me,'' Morgan said a little too briskly, ''and I do. I don't want you to get sick on me. I didn't carry you all the way back here just to have you come down with pneumonia.''

He'd told her that before, but his words seemed to suddenly fall into place. He had actually carried her back. In the storm. The vision was hopelessly romantic. And yet she refused to accept it as such. She couldn't be having romantic notions. Not about Morgan. And she engaged, for heaven's sake. Or almost engaged. She'd made up her mind to tell Daniel yes.

Hadn't she?

Traci tried to prop herself up on her elbows, but the effort was too much for her. Weakly, she sank down against the sofa.

"You carried me all the way?" It had to be, what, at least a mile from the bridge to the house? Maybe two. She wasn't any good at gauging distances and she wasn't very good at gauging what was going on inside her right now, either. She didn't know what to say.

Morgan maintained a stony expression. "I thought of dragging you by one foot, but then you would have gotten mud in your hair and I would have never heard the end of it."

The answer made her smile. "I guess a little of me has rubbed off on you over the years."

He shivered in response, then deadpanned, "Horrible, isn't it? I'm seeing about having it surgically removed. In the meantime, we've got to get you into some dry clothes."

He'd saved her life once, maybe twice if she stretched it, and they'd known each other forever, but there was a place to draw the line and it was here.

"Not 'we,' Morgan. This isn't a joint project." This time she managed to get herself into a sitting position. But not without a price. Pins and needles attacked her from all angles, all aimed at the bump on her head. "Ow." Her hand automatically flew to her forehead. The lump beneath the bandage felt as if it were the size of a melon. "Oh, heck, maybe it is a joint project, after all."

Right now, she didn't feel as if she could even stand by herself.

"Be still my beating heart."

His tone was softer than she thought it would be. Traci looked at him, wondering what he was thinking and if what had happened just before she'd left was somehow coloring everything for Morgan. It certainly was for her, even though she was steeped in pain and clutching on to denial with both hands.

Much as the idea of peeling her clothes off for her appealed to him, Morgan knew that in his present state of mind, it was tantamount to playing with fire.

"I think you can manage, given time," he assured her. But what to put on was the problem. "I don't suppose you brought a change of clothes with you?"

She began to shake her head and then stopped. "No." She breathed the word out heavily. "Why should I?"

It had only been a shot in the dark. "Good point, but then, you've never conformed to the norm. Nothing wearable in the car at all?"

Morgan was thinking along the lines of a castoff sweatshirt or sweatpants Traci might have tossed into the car after a workout at her health club. Traci had always been gung ho for physical fitness and liked exercising with people around. He preferred working out in solitude in his own garage.

Traci sighed. "Not unless I feel like wearing

spark plugs and trying out for Ms. Toolbelt of 1997.''

"You wouldn't win," he commented. "You don't have the injectors for it."

She wondered if that was a veiled comment about her chest. She'd always been small, or, as she preferred thinking of it, "athletically built." The idea that she was wondering if he was thinking about her bra size at all told her that she'd gotten more shaken up in the accident than she'd thought.

"And what's that supposed to mean?"

"Nothing." He rose to his feet. What he needed, he thought, was some distance between them so he could sort out these very odd feelings he was having. "It just sounded like some inane thing you'd say to me." He squared his shoulders. "I've got a flannel shirt upstairs. I guess that'll have to do."

She didn't understand. Her mind kept drifting. Had he always been this good looking? "Do? Do for what?"

"For you to change into," he said patiently, slowly, as if he were speaking to someone whose brain had been dropped in a blender. "Until your clothes dry. I can hang them out here by the fire." He nodded toward the fireplace.

She stared at the empty, dark hearth. "There isn't one."

"I'll make it."

In all the years she'd been coming here, they hadn't once used the fireplace. She'd always wondered what it would look like with a big, roaring fire blazing in it. "Do you know how?"

She really did think of him as inept, didn't she? "Yes, I know how." He began to back out of the room. "Now let me go get that shirt for you. You see if you can conserve your energy for a while— by not talking."

She wanted to get up and show him that she was fine. But her stubborn streak went only so far. Her energy deserted her and she sank back against the sofa. Damp or not, the cushions felt good beneath her. "Knew you were going to say that."

He laughed. "If you didn't, then I really would be worried that you hit your head too hard." Morgan paused, looking at her, then crossed back to the sofa. He looked down into her eyes.

Traci felt as if she were lying on a science lab table, about to be dissected. She tried to look indignant. "What are you doing?"

Very carefully, Morgan looked from one eye to the other. "Checking the size of your pupils."

Somewhere in the back of her mind, Traci recalled mismatched pupils were a sign that a person had a concussion. "Why, Morgan, you say the sexiest things."

He wondered how incapacitated she'd have to be before she stopped talking. "I want to see if they're both the same size."

She waved him back. "You've been watching too many medical programs."

"Maybe, but you'd be surprised what you can

pick up." Satisfied, he backed away again. "You're okay." Then he grinned. "Or as okay as you can be."

"Thank you, Dr. Brigham. Does the AMA know you're practicing without a license?"

"Only on guinea pigs," he retorted as he left the room.

She opened her mouth to answer his retort and found that she couldn't think of a damn thing. She was too tired to be irritated by it.

He had rescued her.

That made it twice in her life, she thought absently. Twice that she was indebted to him. Who would have ever thought that her personal Sir Lancelot was a man she was destined to fight with every time they were in the same room together?

Well, maybe not every time, she mused. Ever so slightly, she skimmed her fingertips over her lips.

Bemused and still very much confused, she sighed. The chill, thanks to her wet clothes, was definitely seeping into her bones. Without thinking, she reached for the crochet afghan that had always lain across the top of the sofa.

But her hand came in contact with only upholstery. Traci looked, even as she remembered that the bright blue-and-gold afghan was now in her parents' den, spread across the sofa there.

She closed her eyes and shivered again. She was just drifting asleep when a hand on her shoulder shook her awake again.

Damn, if she did have a head injury, he

couldn't let her fall asleep. He had to keep her up a few hours. This particular piece of insight came from the same program she'd just ridiculed, but he had no doubt that it was accurate.

Morgan shook her shoulder again, less gently. "Here, take this."

She pried her eyes open. This time was a lot easier than the last had been, but it was still annoyingly painful.

Morgan was standing before her, a glass of water in one hand and a couple of aspirins in the palm of his other. A blue-and-white flannel work shirt was slung over one forearm.

"What's this?" she murmured, bracing herself as she sat up. Though it was cold, she could feel a light sheen of perspiration forming along her forehead and beneath the bandage.

"Aspirin. I figure you probably have one hell of a headache." He sat down carefully beside Traci and offered the pills to her.

Without thinking, she leaned her shoulder against him as she took the aspirins and then the glass of water. "I do." She swallowed, then looked at him as she returned the glass. "Thanks. Is it my imagination, or have you gotten more thoughtful?"

He took the glass from her, placing it on the scarred coffee table. Morgan debated putting his arm around her, purely for reasons of comfort, and then decided not to. No sense testing new ground at the moment.

"Neither. I've always been thoughtful. You just never noticed."

"Thoughtful," Traci repeated slowly. The word evoked scenes in her mind that were completely to the contrary. "Was that when you glued together my sheets with bubble gum, or when you—"

He knew she could go on forever if he let her. "That was only in retaliation for things you did. I never started any of it on my own." He waited for her to deny it, even though it was true. When she didn't say anything, he smiled. "Got you, don't I?"

For the moment, she was forced to concede. "Until I can come back with an answer. That smack to my forehead has made things a little fuzzy." She saw the look that entered his eyes and it touched her. "Don't look so concerned, I was just speaking figuratively." She pointed to the shirt on his arm. "Is that what I'm supposed to wear?"

Morgan nodded, passing the shirt to her. Traci held it up against herself. It looked like an abbreviated nightshirt. She could remember a time when they were almost the same height, but in the past fifteen years, he had outdistanced her by a foot.

Traci laughed, some of her steadiness returning. "How chic. Our mothers would have a heart attack."

He didn't know about hers, but his would have probably been overjoyed, and hoping for more.

But then, his mom had belonged to a commune or something like that in her late teens and he'd been convinced that there was something a little unorthodox about her.

"Our mothers are highly practical women who know the value of warm clothes and dry feet." He gestured toward the bathroom. "Get changed."

"Right." She rose to her feet and the room followed. At an angle. "Whoa." Traci felt behind her for the sofa and found Morgan instead. She landed in his lap. "Nice catch."

He shook his head. Everything was a joke with her. Or an argument. He wondered if there was any middle ground. "I keep in shape. Are you all right? Do you want to lie down some more? I can take you up to your room," he offered.

She didn't like being fussed over. "I'm fine." With renewed determination, she stood again. "Just let me get my sea legs."

This time, he rose with her. Just in case. "We're on land, Traci."

The man was a stickler for precision, she thought. A little like Daniel. Except different. Very different. "Then just let me get my land legs." Traci exhaled, leaning against him without meaning to. Realizing that she was, she straightened and then took a deep, cleansing breath. "Better. All right, let me change into this little number before my sanity returns."

He watched her leave the room, knowing that

to offer any more help would be leaving himself
open to another duel of words.

"Small chance of that," he commented. "It
hasn't made an appearance in all the years I've
known you."

She looked at him over her shoulder, a grin
playing along her lips. "Flatterer."

She was going to be okay, he thought.

When she returned to the living room, Morgan
was busy stoking the fire. To her amazement, he
had a healthy-sized blaze going in the hearth, just
like the one she'd fantasized about in her
imagination.

Barefoot, she padded over to Morgan and,
standing behind him, she let the warm glow from
the fireplace graze her skin. As the only source of
warmth in the room, it felt wonderful.

Or almost the only source of warmth in the
room, she amended, looking down at the back of
Morgan's head.

He sensed her entrance as soon as she walked
into the room. For once, she wasn't talking, but
he knew she was there just the same.

Morgan could feel nerve endings coming to attention all along his body, especially when she
carelessly brushed her bare leg against his arm a
moment before she crouched down beside him.
To keep himself sane, he began mentally catalog-
ing her vices.

He didn't get very far, even though he told
himself there was a host to choose from.

Traci tried not to dwell on how romantic it all seemed.

"So, you really do know how to make a fire. And all these years, I thought of you as a klutz." She spread her hands out before the fire, palms up, letting the heat glaze over them. "It feels better already."

Morgan rose, moving away from her. Staying too close was only inviting the kind of trouble he wasn't prepared to deal with.

He looked toward the window. There was nothing to look at. For all intents and purposes, they might as well have been the last two people in the world.

Now there was a sobering thought. He felt her eyes on him and nodded toward the window. "The storm's getting worse."

She came to stand beside him, suddenly feeling very isolated. "That means we're stuck here for the night?"

He thought of the two disabled cars and the phone that didn't work. "Looks that way."

She blew out a breath, hoping he wouldn't notice how nervous the thought made her. "Lovely."

Something nudged at him. He refused to recognize it as jealousy because then he'd know that he had really gone over the deep end. "Daniel waiting for you?"

"Daniel's at a convention," she said absently. It looked like the end of the world out there. Just how isolated were they out here? When she'd spent summers here, the town had been little less than a handful of stores and a garage. She hoped it had built up since then. "He won't be back until Sunday night." She turned to look at Morgan. "What are we going to do for food?" Except for a granola bar in the car, she hadn't eaten since early this morning.

"I brought some up with me this morning."

She looked at him curiously.

"I was planning to stay the weekend."

Relieved, Traci followed him to the kitchen and watched as Morgan opened the refrigerator to show her it wasn't empty. There were several items on the glass racks and there was a bottle of wine on the top shelf.

Traci turned amused eyes toward Morgan. "Were you planning on spending it drunk?"

"No." He shut the door again, then leaned his back against it, studying her. "I thought of toasting the old place one last time. With you if you wanted to. Alone if you didn't."

"Very thoughtful." She grinned. "There's that word again."

Morgan turned to look at her. He was making her feel very uneasy, looking at her that way. She suddenly wished she'd thought to comb her hair or maybe put on a fresh layer of lipstick. She probably looked like something the cat dragged in.

So what? This was Morgan, remember?

That was just the trouble, she did remember. All the way back to the front door and the kiss that had subversively changed her feelings about a lot of things.

She gestured toward the refrigerator. "Well, bring it out." Traci looked down at the flannel shirt that skimmed the middle of her thighs. "I'm as ready as I'll ever be, I guess."

For what? The question came from nowhere and he knew the sort of answer he wanted to give. He'd never seen his work shirt look so good before, he mused. On her it wasn't just a comfortable yard of material. It was sensuously enticing. He watched the way the hem moved back and forth along her soft skin and it made him envious of a bolt of cloth.

He shoved his hands into his pockets before he did something stupid, like drag her into his arms and kiss her again. "Don't you think that you should have something to eat first?"

Eating, right. What was she thinking? She knew exactly what she was thinking—of making love with Morgan. Of seeing if those bells, banjos and whatnots would show up again.

"When did you get this mothering nature?"

Here he was, mentally stripping away the flannel shirt from her body inch by torturous inch, and there she was, calling him maternal. He should have his head examined.

Morgan pulled open the refrigerator door. "Fine, suit yourself—"

She hadn't meant to insult him. Heaven help her, she actually liked the fact that he worried about her. What was the matter with her?

"Something to eat would be nice," she answered airily. "What do you have?"

He opened the refrigerator again to show her. "Eggs, bread. Ham." There was some mayonnaise in the pantry as well as a children's breakfast cereal that he had never managed to outgrow.

She nodded, hardly hearing. "Sounds good. I'll do the honors."

He took out a frying pan and placed it on the stove. "You cook?"

She took the handle of the pan and moved it to another burner. "There is no end to my talents, Morgan." Taking out the carton of eggs, she shut the door with her hip. The edge of the work shirt hiked up on her thigh. "How do you like them?"

You don't want to know. It took a moment before he could tear his eyes away from her legs. The last time he'd seen them that exposed, they'd been toothpicks. They certainly weren't now. "Whatever's easy."

She had to get past this sizzling feeling in her veins, Traci told herself. This was Morgan. Morgan, not a hunk centerfold of the month.

But it might have been. He certainly looked good enough to be one.

"Easy it is."

Expertly, she cracked four eggs against the side of the skillet and deposited them one at a time into the pan. Eggs were her specialty. Actually, eggs were the only thing she could make with confidence, but she wasn't about to tell him that.

When she popped four slices of toast into a

very dusty looking toaster, the fluorescent lights overhead began to wink.

"Uh-oh, something tells me I'd better make this quick." The thought of being stranded here in the dark was less than pleasing. "You have candles?"

Morgan was already opening the drawers housed beneath the counter. There were three in a row. The first two were empty, except for a few dead insects. "That's what I'm looking for."

The last drawer yielded only one candle. A further search of the kitchen didn't add to the booty. Morgan laid the candlestick on the table. "I've got a flashlight in my car. You stay here, I'll go get it."

The idea of being left behind didn't appeal to her. Neither did the idea of having Morgan go off alone. Not when the weather resembled something Noah must have experienced as he loaded two of everything onto the ark. What if Morgan couldn't find his way back?

"How long will you be gone?"

He detected a nervous note in her voice and interpreted it his own way. "Don't worry, I'm not about to hitchhike into town and leave you." He wondered if there was any sense in putting his jacket on. It was still soaked. "I doubt that anyone is going to be out in this."

She frowned. Was it her, or had the wind gotten louder? "I wasn't thinking of your leaving me. I was worried that you might get lost." She thought of calling him a few choice things for even think-

ing of going out in this, but knew it was futile.
He was as stubborn as she was when it came to
taking advice. "Take the dog with you," she
added suddenly.

Morgan walked into the living room. Jeremiah
was stretched out before the hearth, a living throw
rug. "Why, so he can bite me? I'd rather do this
alone, thanks."

She sighed, her fears multiplying. Well, if he
wanted to go out in this, that was his choice.

Traci turned on her heel and returned to the
kitchen. "You're as stubborn as you ever were."

"Thanks." His voice drifted back to her.

In the kitchen, she braced her shoulders as she
heard the front door slam shut. It took her pre-
cisely two seconds to make up her mind. Shoving
the skillet onto the side of the stove, she raced to
the door, unmindful of the fact that, except for the
nightshirt, she was barefoot up to the neck.
Throwing open the door, she was all set to run
after him.

Her body slammed into his. Morgan was still
standing on the front porch.

Amusement whispered over his features as his
eyes washed over her. "You always run out barefoot into a storm like that?"

The creep. He knew why she'd gone running
out like this. Words tumbled out after one another
without thought. "Only when I'm running after
an idiot. You're not going to find the car. It's
pitch-black out and you'll get lost. You've got the
sense of direction of a dead frog."

He placed a hand over his heart. "I'm touched." And he was, although he wasn't about to say it. Not yet. Not until he understood what was happening here.

"I don't want to have to explain this to your mother," she muttered, utilizing the excuse he'd given her earlier. "Hard as it is to believe, she's attached to you." As was she, Traci added silently.

He glanced back at the inclement weather. His sense of direction was a good deal keener than she speculated, but he didn't think he could find the cars easily.

"Hard as it is to believe," Morgan echoed, "you actually make sense. I might lose my way in this." He sighed, ushering her back inside. "I guess we're just going to have to stay around the fireplace if the lights go out."

Just as the door closed behind them, the lights went out. She turned, her head brushing against his chest. "You were saying?"

"Fireplace it is." Taking her arm, he guided her back into the living room. "What about the eggs?"

"Fortunately, they're ready. I'll go get them." Leaving his side, she shivered.

He thought of putting his arm around her, then decided against it. In her present condition, she might just bite it off.

"I think there are still a couple of blankets in the hall closet," he remembered. "I'll get them."

"Thanks."

He paused, watching as she walked off to the kitchen. The light from the fireplace wrapped itself around her silhouette and did very strange things to the condition of his gut.

Morgan blinked and forced himself to fetch the blankets.

7

Traci pushed aside her empty plate on the hearth. Because of the damp chill throughout the house, she and Morgan had opted to eat on the floor before the fireplace.

Jeremiah came instantly to attention. He trotted

over to the plate and began licking it, obviously picking up some of the flavor of the scrambled eggs. She'd left some toast behind for him to dispose of as well, even though, for lack of anything better, Morgan had given the dog a ham sandwich.

"I guess it beats having a dishwasher," Morgan commented, setting his own plate down beside hers on the floor.

"No matter how good his food is, or how full he gets, I've found that Jeremiah always likes what I'm eating better." She shifted so that she could face Morgan. It wasn't that easy a maneuver, given her present outfit. "You wouldn't have any popcorn around, would you?"

Morgan looked at the dog, then at Traci. "I guess foraging must run in the family." Tension and scrambled eggs had been enough to fill him up. "You're still hungry?"

She frowned at her plate, now completely cleaned. Jeremiah was working on the flowery design. "This wasn't exactly a gourmet seven-course meal we just had."

On the floor, Morgan leaned his back against the sofa. "I'm full."

She sniffed. As if that was supposed to make a difference. "You probably had lunch. Besides, I thought making popcorn would give us something to do. There's no radio or TV and it's only six o'clock."

He looked at his wristwatch, angling the face

so that he could get enough light to read it. "More like seven."

Seven. She could remember when her evenings didn't even start until nine.

"Boy, time sure flies when you're having fun." Content to let Jeremiah amuse himself with the plates, she settled back beside Morgan. If it was actually close to seven, that meant she was missing a chunk of time. Her eyes narrowed. "How long was I out when you brought me back?"

Fear had blanketed him when he hadn't been able to rouse her. "Long enough to make me worry."

Pulling on the hem of the shirt, she shifted around further and stared at him in surprise. "Were you? Really? Worried about me?"

The thought evoked a warm, shimmery feeling throughout her body that Traci wasn't certain if she wanted to savor or push aside. For now, she merely explored it. It did feel nice.

He didn't want her making too much of his admission and using it to his disadvantage. "Traci, I would have worried about a complete stranger I dragged out of a wreck. I am human, you know."

Stupid to think he'd actually meant something by it. Her smile faded as she turned her face from him. "Sorry, didn't mean to tread on your humanity."

He noted the hurt in her voice. It was slight, but he was certain it was there. For once, he hadn't meant to wound her pride.

"Besides," he went on, "we do go back a long way and I do care about you—I guess."

Renewed interest entered Traci's eyes when she looked at him. "You guess?"

For the life of him, he couldn't read the look on her face. "Sure, the same way I care about your mother and father. And Mr. McGillis." How stupid could he get, pulling that out of the air? he upbraided himself.

So much for thinking that he was trying to tell her something. "Mr. McGillis?"

"My mailman."

"Oh."

She looked toward the kitchen. The rooms were arranged so that they all fed into one another, all appearing to share common ground. There was enough light for her to wash the dishes if she was so inclined. At the moment that didn't seem like such a bad idea. She needed some distance between them.

But when she began to rise, she found that there wasn't a ladylike way to manage it.

She tugged at the hem of his shirt again, exasperated. "You know, this isn't the easiest trick, keeping this down to acceptable lengths."

He had to stop looking at her legs, he admonished himself. Out loud, he was the essence of nonchalance. "I've seen you naked before."

"I was six, you were eight."

He shrugged, allowing his eyes to elaborately slip over her body. Was it his imagination, or was it getting increasingly harder to maintain his poise? "Not much difference."

Traci clenched her teeth together and tugged at the hem again, beginning to rise. "Thanks."

"Don't mention it." He noted the losing battle she was waging. "You pull on that any harder, and it's going to tear."

She let out a loud sigh and sank back down. The hell with the dishes. "This is payback time, isn't it?"

He hadn't the slightest clue was she was driving at. "Payback?"

"For the time I stole your clothes when you were skinny-dipping."

She'd yanked them from the bushes where he'd had everything spread out and had run, laughing, into the house. Morgan had finally entered an hour later, holding two branches around himself. One had turned out to be poison oak. Guilt ridden, Traci had stayed up, helping him apply salve to the blisters that were accessible until his parents and hers had returned from the party next door.

That had been the first time he'd witnessed any compassion in her. And just possibly the only time, until today when he had told her about Cynthia.

"If you mean that I arranged the storm, the bridge washing out and the tree being in a place where you would back up into it, you're giving me just a little more credit than I deserve."

He was being deliberately obtuse. "I mean the clothes."

It wasn't easy keeping the smile from his lips, but he managed. "Check my closet. There's nothing there."

She didn't have to look to know it was empty. That wasn't the point.

"But you're wearing dry pants." She dared him to deny that he had completely changed his clothes before coming down with the shirt he'd given her. "I distinctly remember that they were wet when you went upstairs."

"I only had one extra pair." He'd packed for a weekend, not for an entire month. "I put it up to a vote and decided that your legs could stand the exposure better than mine could."

"A vote?" she echoed, confused. "Who voted?"

"Me," he answered innocently. "And since possession is nine-tenths of the law, I figure that tipped the scale in my favor." Affably, he unnotched his belt and slipped the tongue from the buckle. "Of course, if you really want me to take them off—"

Her hand flew out to stop him. "No!" Traci shook her head vehemently, then moaned. The playful exchange stopped.

Morgan leaned forward, feeling damn helpless. "Bad?"

Traci bit her lower lip. She hadn't meant to let the sound escape, but the pain had caught her by surprise. "I wouldn't even wish this on you."

"You're getting me really worried, Traci." Morgan rose, looking toward the door. The storm hadn't let up, but there were worse things than braving a storm. "Look, maybe it's not my distributor cap. Maybe it's something else. If I can fool around with the engine—"

Startled, Traci was up on her knees. He couldn't be serious. "In a monsoon?"

Annoyance at his own helplessness added a sharp edge to his answer. "Do you have any better ideas?"

"Yes." When he looked at her expectantly, her mouth softened into an inviting smile. "Just sit down and talk to me."

"I don't see how—"

She wrapped her fingers around his hand and tugged him back down. "You wouldn't, but fortunately you don't have to."

Her smile chased away some of the tension he was feeling—or at least, the tension related to worry. The tension that was related to the sexual disquietude weaving back and forth between them only intensified.

"The sound of your voice makes me feel better." She wondered if she was going to regret admitting that. Probably. "I guess it must all be part of that blow to the head."

"Must be." Relenting, he got comfortable and then surprised them both by slipping his arm around her shoulders. "Still cold?"

She shivered, but this time it wasn't from the chill. Anticipation rippled through her. Traci tried vainly to relax.

"Not anymore." Nerves played leapfrog within

her and she hadn't a viable explanation as to why. "That's a nice fire," she whispered, wishing she wasn't feeling so incredibly fidgety.

"Thanks."

He stared into the flames. He felt it was safer than looking at her. Or allowing himself to smell her hair, or think how soft her body might feel beneath his shirt.

The glow from the hearth did a decent job of lighting the room. Shadows reached out along the walls and ceiling in vague, undefined shapes.

Rather like the feelings that were racing through him, he mused.

"It's kind of eerie, though," he commented.

She stared at the shadows, at the way the light played with them. There was a time she would have seen monsters in every shape. But she'd come a long way from that little girl.

Or so she liked to think.

"Oh, I don't know," she mused loftily. "With the right kind of mind-set, you might even call this romantic." Too late, she realized her mistake. Traci looked at Morgan. She didn't want him misunderstanding. "With the right person, I mean."

"Absolutely," he agreed softly. "With the right person."

His eyes were on hers and she could feel his touch, though he hadn't moved an iota since placing his arm around her. Her nerves were growing at a disproportionate rate. "Not the two of us," she felt compelled to say.

Desire, strong and urgent, was making an unexpected appearance and it was all he could do to keep from kissing her. "Are you that sure?"

"Of course I'm sure." Her voice broke and she cleared her throat.

What the hell was the matter with her? She'd come up here to sort out her feelings about Daniel, not pick up new ones about Morgan. But she couldn't think when he was looking at her like that. Like someone she didn't know. Like someone she wanted to know.

Traci looked away. "Oh, you mean what happened earlier. Well, that was your fault."

He didn't think he'd ever seen her nervous before. "I don't think the word *fault* is the right one in this case."

She continued staring into the flames. Her nerves refused to settle down. "Well, whatever you want to call it, it was an aberration." Gathering her courage to her, she turned to look at him, her eyes daring him to dispute her words. "Like Halley's comet falling."

Satisfaction lit his eyes and curved his mouth. "Felt that way to you, too, did it?"

This conversation wasn't going the way she wanted it to. She pulled away from him. "I'm going to get some wine."

Morgan watched in fascination as Traci rose to her feet. For once, he forgot to be a gentleman. Damn, but she had turned out to be a beautiful figure of a woman.

"Why?" he called after her.

"Because you're out of popcorn." She disappeared into the kitchen.

Morgan heard the refrigerator door being opened and then slammed shut. He looked at the dog who, finished scavenging, was curled up on the far side of the hearth. "She's gotten harder to follow, hasn't she?"

Jeremiah didn't bother lifting his head. He opened his eyes and looked with disinterest at Morgan for a moment before his lids slid shut again.

Traci entered the room, the bottle tucked under her arm and two mugs plus the corkscrew he'd brought with him in her hands. Kneeling down, she folded her legs under her before offering the mugs to Morgan.

"We're going to have to toast each other with these. I can't find any glasses." She placed the bottle between them.

"Glasses." Morgan shook his head at his oversight. Somehow, drinking out of mugs just wasn't the same. "I knew I forgot something."

"You forgot extra clothes," she accused. Glasses didn't matter. Dignity, however, did. Holding the hem of the shirt down again, she rearranged her legs.

He caught a glimmer of her thigh where the shirt had risen. He couldn't find it in his heart to regret the oversight on his part. "Sue me."

The lawyer's answer to everything, she mused. "Don't tempt me."

He grinned at her just before he sank the tip of the corkscrew into the cork. "Ditto."

He thought she blushed, but it might just have been the light from the fire washing over her face. Still, he had his doubts. Morgan twisted the corkscrew in and then pulled.

Traci kept her eyes fixed on the mug as he poured, afraid to look at him. Was he telling her that he was being tempted by her? Or was this just his attempt at wry wit?

She didn't know and she was afraid to speculate.

Morgan filled Traci's mug halfway, then poured a like amount into his own. He lifted his mug toward her and the fireplace. "To the house."

She touched the side of her mug to his. "And to memories."

Their eyes held for a long moment before she brought her mug to her lips.

The wine aroused her sensations, just as the look on his face aroused her. She needed something else to concentrate on.

Traci took another long sip, then studied her mug. "Not bad."

The warmth the liquid spread over her limbs was pleasing. For a moment, it nudged aside the other warmth that was zipping erratically through her, popping up and down like beads of water on a hot skillet.

Desperate to drown it out completely, Traci

drank the rest of her wine, then presented the mug to Morgan for a refill.

"Go easy," he warned, pouring.

She didn't need him telling her how to behave. And she didn't need him looking at her like that, either. Least of all, she didn't need him kissing her.

Or did she?

She raised her chin. "You think I don't know when to stop?"

None of his business how much she downed. "Sorry, don't know what came over me to suggest that."

Morgan set the bottle down on the stone hearth before them, then savored his own drink. Somehow, he'd lost his taste for it. He looked at her, watching the way the flames caressed her face. Wishing he could do the same.

"So, you're really getting married to this Daniel guy?"

She was already starting to feel the effects of the first mug as she began to make short work of the second. Her head was spinning, but that didn't change anything. She still felt an uneasiness inside of her. And a new hunger she didn't know what to do with.

"Yup, I'm really getting married to this Daniel guy," she snapped.

That wine tasted awfully good. She had had no idea she was this thirsty. Draining the mug, Traci reached for the bottle.

"Traci, I don't think you should be drinking this much."

"Much?" she repeated, struggling not to slur the word. "You think this is much? You, sir, have no idea what much is."

Did she have a problem with alcohol? He tended to doubt it, but it might have slipped by both their parents' detection. Very deliberately, Morgan placed his hand on the bottle and took it from her. "You don't do this all the time, do you?"

She pressed her lips together. Did he think she was some kind of wino? She didn't even know why she was doing this now. Maybe because what she was feeling was easier to tolerate when the wine blurred the edges from it.

Holding the mug in both hands, she sighed. "I can't remember the last time I had a glass of wine."

He moved the bottle behind him. "Maybe that's because your mind's getting foggy again."

"Nope, it's clear as glass," she declared, taking another long sip. And then his question about her marrying Daniel came echoing back at her, as if she hadn't answered it at all. But she had, hadn't she?

She wasn't sure. Testing her tongue, she voiced her thoughts aloud. Maybe if she heard them, she would believe them. "You know, Daniel's very nice."

Morgan studied her expression. Inebriated or

not, she was trying to say something that wouldn't come out. "But?"

Traci blinked, looking at him. "But what?"

He shook his head. When she raised the mug to her lips, he placed his hand over her wrist, guiding it back down to her side. He wanted her to finish what she was trying to tell him.

"No, you have a 'but.'"

She glanced down. It took her a moment to focus her eyes. Her mouth spread in a wide smile as laughter threatened to bubble up in her chest. "Yes, I do. It makes sitting easier."

He laughed, then shook his head. She raised her eyes to his face questioningly. The lady, he thought, was on her way to being smashed.

"In your sentence," he prodded. "You had a 'but' in your sentence."

She thought for a moment, remembered and then opted for denial. "No, I didn't."

Morgan saw the defensiveness kick in as if it were a physical thing. "Be honest, Traci."

For a moment, she sobered. Loyalty to Daniel warred with her true feelings. "Do I have to?"

His voice softened as he moved closer to her. "Makes things easier."

If he only knew. "Not from where I'm sitting." She sighed again, leaning back, not completely aware that she was leaning into Morgan, as well. She thought of Daniel. Sweet, patient Daniel. He deserved someone who could love him the way he should be loved, not by half measures. "He's everything a woman could want."

That was a party line, Morgan knew, not her true feelings. The small kernel of jealousy he'd felt earlier fell through the cracks and disappeared.

"But?" he prodded gently.

She looked at him and bit her lip. The truth came before she could lock it away. Someone had to know. "He doesn't make the bells and the banjos play for me." *Like you do.*

He thought he understood, but he wasn't quite sure. "And having an orchestra around is important to you?"

"Yes."

Reaching around him, she secured the bottle and wrapped her fingers around its neck. Traci drew it to her and poured a little more of the rose-colored liquid into her mug. But instead of drinking it, she stared into the container, as if seeing things there that would quell her troubled soul.

"There's no music without one. No chemistry. No fire." She raised her eyes to his. "There's even chemistry when I look at you and you're not as good-looking as Daniel is."

She really was getting smashed, he thought. Gingerly, he took the mug away from her, surprised at how easily she surrendered it. "Thanks."

"No," she said, not wanting him to get the wrong idea. "You're cute. Maybe you're even gorgeous, but your nose is a little crooked."

She really was pretty adorable this way, he

mused. If he wasn't careful, he'd let himself get carried away. "You broke it, remember?"

Yes, she remembered. Remembered swinging the door into his face. But it had been an accident. She hadn't known Morgan was behind her. And he hadn't stopped walking in time.

"You were always such a klutz." Traci smiled fondly. Her eyes narrowed as she took further inventory of his face. "And your mouth's a little too full."

As if to give it a stamp of approval despite that fact, she leaned over and kissed him. Surprising the hell out of him.

As he reached for her, she moved her head back. She gave it a smart nod. "But it does taste good." She ran her tongue over her lower lip, sampling. "You been drinking?"

"Just a little." He didn't want to laugh at her, but it wasn't easy. "Traci, I think that you've had a little too much."

"No, I haven't." She looked around for her mug. It was here somewhere. She remembered holding it, or at least she thought she did. "I'm still trying to make the bells and the banjos go away."

She was rambling, but he humored her. "I thought you said you wanted them."

"With Daniel." Her eyes looked into his. Didn't he understand? "Not with you."

He wondered if his mouth was hanging open. It sure felt that way. "With me?"

She nodded, then blinked hard because there

were two of him. She waited until the images merged. They did, but only partially. "Stop moving around so much. You're vibrating."

Yes, he probably was at that, he thought. Morgan took her hands into his. A thousand thoughts ran through his mind, like field mice scurrying for high ground during a flash flood. He had to have misheard her.

"You hear those bells and banjos with me?"

"I think so." Right now, she wasn't certain of anything. "Only one way to make sure." Taking his face between her hands, she kissed him. Hard. As if everything depended on it.

He didn't mean to kiss her back, knew that if nothing else, he was taking advantage of the situation. And of her. She was obviously feeling no pain right now and he should be stepping back.

But it was more than he could resist. She was more than he could resist.

At least for a moment.

Her mouth was so eager, so giving, and her body so soft against his. He felt his own head reeling as he deepened the kiss, meeting her more than halfway and getting lost in the process so that he couldn't begin to find his way back.

He wanted to make love with her. To strip away the games they'd both been playing all these years and all day. He wanted her the way he'd never wanted any other woman. His hands felt as if they were trembling as he reached for the button at her throat and began to push it through the tiny hole.

Beneath his fingers, he could feel the swell of her breasts as she caught her breath.

This was wrong. He couldn't do this, not when she was so intoxicated. What if it was only the wine talking and not her?

Digging deep for strength, Morgan took hold of her arms and held her back.

"See?" she asked huskily. "Bells and banjos. Can't you hear them?"

He did, he thought. He really did. She was scrambling his brain.

Traci didn't wait for his answer. She clutched at his shirt. "Make them stop, Morgan. I can't have them playing when I'm kissing you. They're supposed to play when I'm kissing Daniel." And then she suddenly paled. Dropping her hands in her lap, Traci began to sway. "Oooh, boy. Suddenly, I don't feel so well."

Was she going to be sick? "Small wonder. I think you'd better get some sleep before I have to pour you into bed." He rose, ready to guide her up the stairs.

But Traci remained where she was. The world was too dark to venture into. She liked it right here, by the fire. And him.

"No, it's dark up there."

Morgan squatted down beside her. "Would you rather sleep down here?"

"Yes." She turned her eyes to his. "With you."

"Um, Traci, it's not that I'm not flattered, but

I really don't think that's such a good idea right now."

But she didn't appear to hear him. Traci was already curling up beside the fire, drawing the blanket around her.

"You can sleep over there and I can sleep here." Traci sighed, getting comfortable. "By the fire. That makes sense, doesn't it?"

Resigned, Morgan smoothed out the other blanket he'd found for them. He thought of sleeping on the sofa, but somehow, it didn't seem right, not with Traci taking the floor. He debated moving her onto the couch, but one look at her had him giving up that idea. She seemed to be completely settled in.

"Whatever you say." This whole visit didn't make sense, but he wasn't about to get into that.

A thought snuck up on her as her eyes were drifting shut. "Morgan?"

He'd just laid down. "Now what?"

"You won't go anywhere, I mean, in the middle of the night, will you?"

The floor was decidedly uncomfortable. He looked toward the sofa, tempted. "Only if I have to."

She didn't like the sound of that. Upset, Traci sat up. The room was reeling, but she held her ground. "What?"

Why was she getting so panicky? "You know, 'have to.' The call of nature," he added when she didn't seem to understand.

"Oh." Relieved, Traci lay back down. "That's okay. Just as long as you don't leave."

"I won't," he promised.

She was asleep before he uttered the last syllable, leaving Morgan to lay awake and stare at the shadows on the ceiling, wondering what the hell he was going to do about this turn of events.

8

Daylight came in with combat boots, stomping around on the hardwood floor like a battalion of marines during basic training maneuvers.

Or was that just Morgan moving around?

Feeling more dead than alive, Traci opened

what she was certain were bloodshot eyes. She was the unhappy owner of a mouth that felt like a bale of cotton.

The light hurt and she automatically shut her eyes down to tiny slits. Only belatedly did she realize that the sun had to be up. Which meant that the storm had to have abated.

But all Traci could think of was that she wished this miserable throbbing would cease.

Sitting up, she held her head and then paused a moment to take in her surroundings. She felt utterly disoriented. She was on the floor, beside a fireplace. The scene had a vaguely familiar feel to it.

Morgan was crouching in front of the fireplace, holding what looked to be a battered, covered pot over the fire.

Focusing hurt.

Traci shut her eyes completely. The moan was involuntary. She could almost literally feel Morgan's eyes on her.

"What did you do to me last night?" Even talking hurt. This was bad. "There are about a thousand little men playing the *Anvil Chorus* in my head."

He didn't envy her the "day after." He'd been there once or twice himself. The only cure was time. And maybe coffee. He was doing his best about that.

"My responsibility ended when I took the bottle away from you." He stared impatiently at the pot he was holding. Damn, this was taking longer than he'd anticipated. He thought that the water would be hot by the time she woke up. "Sorry I can't offer you coffee yet, but the power's still out."

With effort, she turned her head toward the window. "The rain's stopped."

The storm had blown over a little after midnight. He'd gone out at first light to check things out and then hiked over to their cars. "I guess maybe He changed His mind about ending the world via flood again."

She didn't hear him. Traci's attention had meandered back to something Morgan had said previously.

"What did you mean, you can't offer me coffee yet?" Right now, she'd kill for just a little of the dark bracing liquid.

"I've been out to the cars." He nodded toward the door. "I picked up some odds and ends to bring back. Your purse, what looks like a portfolio, my flashlight and some instant coffee."

She would have commented on the portfolio and his thoughtfulness if the coffee hadn't been of eminent importance to her at the moment. "Where did you get instant coffee?"

He gave the pot another shake, as if that would somehow speed up the process. "As it happens, I had some in my car."

She dragged her hand through her hair, trying to make sense out of what she was hearing. Her hair hurt. If she concentrated, she could feel every follicle. "You carry instant coffee around in your car?"

"It came in my morning mail. A free sample." Morgan looked over his shoulder at the packet he'd dropped on the coffee table beside her purse. "I tossed my mail into the car, thinking I'd look at it later. I forgot about the sample until I went to get the flashlight." He looked at the dog that was sitting beside him. Jeremiah's head was resting regally on outstretched paws. "Took your dog out for a walk while I was at it. You know, he's not half-bad once he settles down."

"I guess the same could be said for you." He had taken her dog out for a walk. And brought back her purse and portfolio. Was this really Morgan? She tried to muster a smile and realized that it hurt the corners of her mouth. Everything felt as if it had been disassembled and then passed through a wringer. She'd never been hung over before, and as far as she was concerned, she didn't see the attraction drinking held if this was what you felt like the next morning.

Her eyes narrowed slightly as she watched him. "What are you doing?"

He grinned at her. "Heating water for your coffee. It's not going to taste very good," he warned, "but at least it'll be hot."

Very gingerly, she got up and crossed to the coffee table. She picked up the small green-and-red packet and turned it over in her hand. The pulsating in her head abated enough for her to be able to read the instructions on the back.

"There's only enough here for one cup." She looked at Morgan. "You're letting me have it?"

He shrugged carelessly. "I figured you need it more than I do."

Moving slowly back to the hearth, she reclaimed her position on the blanket on the floor. "Very chivalrous of you. Your list of good qualities is growing."

A half smile curved his mouth. "So you mentioned last night."

Last night. What else had she said to him last night? Traci tried to remember, but it was all a hazy, vague fog. Snippets drifted through her mind. She prayed she hadn't made a fool of herself.

She glanced toward him. Was that a smug expression on his face? "About last night…"

A well-shaped, dark brow arched in her direction. "Yes?"

She couldn't bluff her way through this. There was nothing else to do but admit the truth. "I don't remember it."

Morgan slowly turned his head to look at her. This had definite possibilities.

Surprise and disbelief entered his eyes. "You mean you really don't remember what amounts to the greatest night in my life?"

Oh, no, what had she done? Fear skittered through her like tiny spiders sliding along a glass-top table.

"No, I—" Traci braced herself for the worst.

Or thought she did. "What happened?" she whispered nervously.

Morgan sat back on his heels. "What didn't?" Admiration filtered through his voice. "I had no idea you were that agile. And with a head injury, too." His eyes skimmed over her, lingering on her long legs. It wasn't difficult adding enthusiasm, not when she looked as tempting as a hot cross bun that had just emerged from the oven. "Why didn't you ever tell me you could bend that way?"

She opened her eyes so wide, her headache intensified another notch. The cottony taste in her mouth threatened to choke her. "What way?"

The smile that slid over his face was sensual enough to have her pulse jumping. "You know."

That was just it, she didn't know. Exactly. But she was afraid that she could make a calculated guess.

Agitated, she rose up to her knees, her hand on his shoulder. "Listen, Morgan, I was under the influence—"

He pretended to be willing to accept that explanation. "If that's the case, maybe I can scrounge up some more around here. I'd hate to think last night was a fluke—"

A fluke. What a funny term for having her life flushed down the toilet. She had to make him understand that it was a mistake. Making love with him—and she was sure that was what he meant— had been a mistake. She couldn't be making love with him when she was almost engaged to Daniel. How had everything gotten so out of hand?

"Whatever happened—I didn't mean for it to happen. I mean—you've got to forget about it." Nerves and throbbing temples made uttering a coherent sentence an unattainable dream. Her mind was running back and forth, unable to get a toehold on anything logical.

He shook his head, his expression solemn. "I doubt I can. Not in a million years."

He fought to hide a grin. Traci looked as if she was going to come unglued right in front of him.

"And if there's a baby—" Morgan began speculatively.

"A baby?"

Her knees gave way and she sank down on the blanket again. She hadn't even thought about that. Traci covered her mouth to smother the squeak of horror bubbling in her throat.

He took her reaction in stride, patiently explaining the situation to her.

"We didn't use any protection. Your purse was still in the car and I didn't think to bring any. Who knew this was going to happen?" No longer hidden, his grin was wider than a Cheshire cat's. "You know, this puts a whole new light on our relationship."

Traci fell over to one side, almost prostrate, on the blanket. She buried her head in the pillow. "There is no relationship. At least, not that way. I think I'm going to be sick."

Morgan set the pot to one side on the hearth

and looked at her. "Why? Is making love with me that repulsive a thought to you?"

With supreme effort, she dragged herself up into a sitting position once more. She really didn't want to hurt his feelings, especially since he was being so nice. But this was an awful mess she had found herself in. She tried to make him understand.

"No, no, it's not. But, Morgan, this wasn't supposed to happen." It had all seemed so simple yesterday morning. How could it have gotten so fouled up in less than twenty-four hours? "I was supposed to come up here, look around, have a few pleasant memories and try to figure out what to do with that engagement ring that's sitting on my kitchen counter." She moaned as she looked at Morgan. "I wasn't supposed to make love with you." Hanging her head, she felt almost desperate. And then she slanted a look at him. "Was it really that good?"

Morgan played it out a little further as he sat down beside her. "There's only one word for it, Traci. Indescribable."

She felt like tearing out her hair. "Then why can't I remember?"

"I don't know." And then the solemn look on his face melted into a wide smile again. "Maybe it's because you passed out."

She couldn't believe what he was admitting to her. Never in a million years would she have thought that Morgan was the kind of man who would force himself on a woman.

"You took advantage of me?"

How could she even think that, no matter how scrambled her brain was? "I covered you."

That wasn't an answer. He was deliberately avoiding her question. "With what," she demanded, incensed, "your body?"

"With a blanket." He tugged at the end of it, catching her off balance. Traci fell over, then scrambled back up to her knees. When she opened her mouth to protest, he told her the truth. "Nothing happened, Traci."

"Nothing?" Her eyes narrowed as she looked at him intently. She'd know if he were lying, she thought. Wouldn't she?

Very calmly, he shook his head. "Nothing."

She thought hard, trying to will last night back in her mind. Only a tiny slice materialized. "But I remember a kiss." She was positive about that. A kiss. A long, warm, lingering kiss.

Caught, Morgan shrugged. "Well, yes, that did happen. But nothing else," he assured her. He thought it best not to point out that she had been the one to kiss him. She probably wouldn't believe him, anyway.

There was still a smidgen of suspicion in her eyes and it annoyed him. She should have known better than to doubt him about something like that. But then, maybe they really didn't know each other any more at that.

"I wasn't about to take advantage of a completely inebriated woman, Traci. If I make love to someone, I expect her to have a clear mind and to remember something beyond the *Anvil Chorus* the next day.''

"Then we didn't—?"

Not that it didn't cross his mind and play havoc with his desire, but he wasn't about to tell her that. "No, we didn't."

Incensed, Traci grabbed the pillow and walloped him with it. "You brute!"

Morgan threw his hands up to ward off the assault, then scrambled up to his feet, nearly upsetting the covered pot behind him. Jeremiah danced out of his way, barking and adding to the commotion.

He stared at her, completely at a loss. "Because I didn't?"

Disgusted, she threw aside the pillow and glared at him. "Because you lied to me."

Peace restored, he reached for the pot. "I was just having a little fun at your expense. You must know what that's like." Jeremiah barked at them again. "Careful," Morgan warned, picking up the coffee sample packet, "my new friend doesn't seem to like you beating me."

Frowning, she rose to her feet. "Traitor," she snapped the accusation at Jeremiah, who whined in response.

It took Traci a minute to calm down. They hadn't made love. It was all a joke. Thank God.

Yeah, thank God.

Everything was all right. So why was she feeling so let down instead of—?

Aspirins, she needed aspirins. And coffee. Hot

coffee, poured straight into her veins. Maybe then she could think straight again.

She looked at Morgan. "Is the water ready yet?"

"Just." He took the mug out of the sink and rinsed it once, then poured the hot water into it. Ripping open the packet of flavored coffee, he added that to the water, then stirred. He brought it back to Traci.

She took the mug in both hands, grateful for something to change the subject. Chagrined, she could still feel her face burning.

Traci took a long sip of coffee, then winced. Nothing would taste good to her right now, she thought. But like Morgan said, it was hot and it was the only thing she had available. She drained the rest of the coffee, then shivered involuntarily. "I think I need a toothbrush."

Morgan took the mug from her, setting it aside on the coffee table. He couldn't help wondering if her violent reaction earlier had been a matter of the lady protesting too much, or if the thought of making love with him had been that repugnant to her. Making love with her wasn't repugnant to him. As a matter of fact, as he sat here near her, the idea was growing on him by the minute.

He wondered what she would say if he told her?

"Mine's upstairs," he told her. "Feel free to use it."

The less they shared, the better. "No thanks, you've put yourself out for me enough as it is."

She ran her tongue over her lower lip, trying to gather her thoughts together. "So, where do we stand?"

He gave her the rundown he'd already been through himself. "The power and the phone are still out, as is the bridge—" The water in the gully was lower this morning and it was only a matter of time before it dissipated altogether, provided it didn't rain again.

She could have sworn that her father had once taken a different route to get here. "Isn't there a long way around out of here?"

He'd taken it several times. "Yes, but it requires a car and we don't seem to have one that's running at the moment." He'd tried to turn his engine over with no luck when he'd gone out for the flashlight. "I thought I'd come back, check on you and then see what I could do with the cars."

He'd never struck her as particularly handy. Changing a light bulb in a ceiling fixture had been a challenge for him when they were younger. When had this transformation happened? "You know how to fix cars?"

"Just a few basic things. I had a client a while back, a mechanic accused of robbing a gas station." Morgan played it down, although he had learned a great deal from Scott. "He couldn't pay me. So I took it out in trade." Morgan shrugged the matter away. "He taught me how to do a few things."

Another man would have just had the mechanic fixing things on his car for him. That Morgan had tried to learn how to do it himself showed Traci a side of him she hadn't thought existed. "Did you win the case?"

Morgan rose, taking her mug with him. "Of course I won."

Traci followed him into the kitchen. "That wasn't a foregone conclusion, was it?"

He didn't mean to make it sound as if he were bragging. "No, but he wouldn't have been able to teach me very much behind bars, now could he?"

He looked at her over his shoulder. She was standing in the doorway, his shirt still swaying gently along her thighs as it settled into place. He felt that same odd tightening in his gut. Best to leave temptation out of the equation. He'd already seen her reaction to having him as a lover.

"Your clothes are dry, by the way, if you want to put them on. Although I have to admit that I rather hate giving up the view."

She felt a warm blush slipping all along her body. He was having fun at her expense again, she thought. Turning on her bare heel, she left for the bathroom to get dressed. "Yeah, right."

"Actually," he said quietly to himself, "it is."

Traci had occupied herself for most of the day by making sketches and plotting further dilemmas for her alter ego to encounter. Toward the end of the afternoon, a new character began taking shape beneath her pencil. A chiseled, strapping repairman who bore a striking resemblance to Morgan.

When she lingered over where his rolled-up shirtsleeves tightened along his biceps, Traci knew she had to take a break.

Morgan had been out of the house for the better part of the afternoon. She knew most of it had been spent working on his car. He'd been right about hers. It was a mangled mess, its bumper crushed up against a tree. It was hard for her to visualize herself in it.

Harder still to visualize Morgan pulling her out of it, then carrying her back here.

But he had.

Very romantic, she thought despite herself. This wasn't helping.

She needed something to contrast his actions with, something to remind her that this was Morgan she was having these feelings about, not some latter-day Lancelot.

Rising, she woke up Jeremiah, who raised his head to watch her go out the front door in search of Morgan. After a moment, he trotted out behind her.

She didn't have far to look.

Morgan was sitting on the front steps of the porch, running a rock over the edge of an ax.

Curious, Traci sat down beside him. The dog planted himself directly behind them. The wood under her jeans was still slightly damp from the rain, but she ignored it.

Traci nodded toward the ax. "What are you doing?"

He'd been trying to talk himself out of these

strange feelings he was having about her all afternoon. It didn't help, having her sit here next to him, smelling sweet and exotic. Stirring him. Didn't that damn perfume of hers ever wear off?

"Sharpening an ax," he answered shortly. "What does it look like I'm doing?"

"Sharpening an ax," she parroted. Traci watched Morgan as his hand moved rhythmically back and forth along the dull blade. "Should I be pushing furniture against the door?"

He spared her a glance. "This isn't *The Shining*. And I'm not Jack Nicholson," Morgan told her glibly, looking back at his work. One slip and he was going to be very unhappy that she had distracted him.

He wasn't particularly overjoyed she was doing it as it was.

Very slowly, she was beginning to feel at ease with him again. Funny how that seemed to be ebbing and receding this weekend. "Very good. You picked up on that."

"I picked up on a lot of things, spending summers around you." There, he thought, that seemed to do the trick. If it didn't, they were going to have to rough it tonight. He had nothing else available to sharpen the ax with.

Morgan rose from the step and headed to the side of the house. "We need firewood for tonight and we're almost all out."

It took her a moment to comprehend. When she did, she was quick to rise to her feet and follow him. "Do I get to watch you chop wood?"

She'd probably feel called upon to narrate the activity, blow by blow, he thought, irritated.

"If you're that bored." Setting a chunk of wood on the stump, Morgan swung down hard. The wood cleaved neatly in half.

Traci watched as Morgan's muscles flexed and relaxed. Just like the character she'd drawn. She tried not to dwell on the comparison.

"Ohh, how primal," she quipped, her eyes lit with amusement. "This must be what Swiss Family Robinson felt like."

He set another chunk of wood on the stump and swung down hard. This time, he mentally tacked a face on the wood. A male face. "That was fiction and they were marooned on an uninhabited island, not in upstate New York."

He seemed particularly short with her. She wondered if it had anything to do with her reaction to what had taken place last night, or rather what she had *thought* had taken place last night.

"You do know how to take the fun out of things, don't you?"

"I try." The sound of ax meeting wood reverberated in the late-afternoon air. He glanced at her as he picked up another piece. "How's your head?"

She'd forgotten about the headache. And the lump beneath the bandage seemed to be shrinking. "Much better, thanks. I think I'll live."

Gritting his teeth, Morgan swung down harder than before. The two pieces flew wildly out. "Daniel will be happy to hear that."

He'd almost spat out Daniel's name. "That's a very disparaging tone," she observed.

Morgan shrugged, then swung. He felt his shoulder muscles protesting. He wasn't accustomed to physical labor in any great amounts. "It's your life."

"Yes, it is." Because she had to do something, she began gathering up the pieces he'd split. "I don't owe you any explanations."

"I'm not asking for any." With a grunt, he swung again. As the pieces fell on either side of the stump, Morgan looked at her. "All right, I am. Why are you throwing away your life on—"

"On what?" she challenged, throwing the two new pieces into the pile against the side of the house. "A successful, kind man?"

"On someone who doesn't make the bells and the banjos play for you," Morgan corrected.

She turned on her heels like someone in a trance. "Who told you that?"

"You did." Another two pieces flew to the ground. "Last night."

She refused to look at him. "That was the wine talking."

He knew better than that. And so did she. "That was the wine *letting* you talk."

She blew out a breath. "All right, if you must know, there was someone before Daniel." She didn't notice the way Morgan's shoulders stiffened. "It didn't last very long. His name was Rory and he was very dynamic, very sexy." She glared at Morgan, her mouth set hard. "The kind of man who could make your toes curl."

Morgan positioned another chunk. "I sincerely doubt that."

"All right, the kind of man who made *my* toes curl." She winced at the sound of the ax meeting wood. "He was exciting and, yes, he made bells and banjos play in my head. He was also a cheating womanizer who left me for someone who could further his career. He was an actor."

Morgan couldn't visualize a man who would willingly turn his back on Traci. "Well, that explains it. He wasn't real."

"Oh, he was real, all right." She tossed the last two pieces on top of the others. "Too real. He left an image in my head that refused to be shut out. Except when—" She stopped.

Morgan stopped swinging. "When—?" he prodded.

She'd said too much already. If he expected her to stand here singing his accolades, he was going to be disappointed.

"Nothing. I'm going inside to see if I can do something creative with ham and eggs. You go on chopping wood." She paused on the steps. "Think the power will be back on tomorrow?"

"At least the phone. That way we can call someone from the town to come get us and our defunct cars." He raised his eyes to hers. "And you can call Daniel."

"Yes, I can," she answered firmly, marching up the stairs again.

She slammed the door in her wake.

"If there was snow on the roof," he commented to Jeremiah, "we would have had an avalanche just then." He rolled the thought over in his head. "I think I would have taken my time before I dug her out."

Jeremiah barked his agreement.

"This is very nice," Morgan commented, taking his seat at the table.

They were eating in the kitchen instead of the living room. There were two candles on the table. They were mismatched, one higher than the other and of a different color, but it didn't matter. Somehow, it seemed right.

"I found a second candle in the attic when I went exploring earlier," she told him. "It had rolled under the old love seat your mother left behind."

"That belonged to your mother," he corrected. They were having cold ham and more scrambled eggs. Traci had cooked them over the fire in the hearth and felt very smug about it.

But she scowled now. "I don't remember ever seeing that at home."

There was a reason for that. "That was because your parents bought that their first summer here." He remembered how his father and hers had struggled, getting the love seat out of the van and up the front steps while their mothers had coached them from the sidelines.

Traci looked ruefully at the mugs filled with

water. Not much of a meal, she mused. "I'm sorry there's no wine tonight."

He smiled, remembering last night. "So am I."

She meant because she'd finished his whole bottle. She had a feeling he meant something else. She looked down at her mug. "At least there's plenty of water."

Outside, it had begun raining again. This time, the sound was gently lulling.

Morgan raised his mug to the sound. "Amen to that."

It sounded, she thought, lifting the mug to her lips, vaguely like a prophesy.

YES, I GAVE DONALD BACK HIS RING. I'M A FREE WOMAN AGAIN AND THIS TIME I INTEND TO STAY THAT WAY.

BUT THAT VCR REPAIRMAN WAS KIND OF CUTE....

9

They lingered over dinner as long as they could, but eventually it was over. The leftovers were awarded to Jeremiah, who disposed of them within a blink of an eye and then lay down to doze by the fire. There weren't many dishes to wash and they were quickly done and put away. There was nothing left to do except to sit by the fire and wait for dawn and, hopefully, restored phone lines.

The evening stretched out endlessly before them. It reminded Traci a little of the first evenings she had spent here with her parents, when she'd bemoaned the lack of a television set and whined that there was nothing to do. But then at least there were other people to talk with and listen to.

There was nothing to do now, either. Except to listen to the beating of her own heart and be acutely aware of the man sitting beside her.

As if to deny his presence, or at least block it out, Traci pulled over her portfolio and took out her sketch pad. Maybe if she got a little more work done, the evening would melt away.

She couldn't think straight.

Exasperated, after a few minutes she set the sketch pad aside on the coffee table. She could feel him looking at her. When she raised her eyes, it was to look directly into his.

Morgan had contented himself with merely watching her; he hadn't said a word. It was his impression that she was only going through the motions. He read between the lines and made his own interpretations.

And came to the same conclusion he had earlier. She was nervous. Something was going on between them and it was barreling toward a showdown, and soon.

It couldn't be soon enough for him. He'd never cared for waiting.

Morgan nodded at the portfolio as she shoved the last of the papers back into it. "I looked over your sketches earlier. While you were in the kitchen."

"Oh?" Belatedly, she remembered her latest sketches. Had he seen himself in the muscular VCR repairman? Traci braced herself for a smug comment.

If he were given to ego, Morgan would have said that the half-finished sketch of the man entering her apartment looked like it was a takeoff on him. But ego wasn't his problem.

She and the feelings she generated were. And he meant to do something about that.

"They look like they have possibilities." Then, because he felt stuck for anything else to say, he added, "I read *Traci on the Spot* every morning before I leave for work."

She really couldn't visualize him taking the time to read a comic strip, at least not one without some sort of political satire attached to it. "Why?"

He had a feeling that she thought he was putting her on. He wasn't. "It helps me see that there's still humor in the world." Due to the nature of the crimes he was forced to face on an almost daily basis, finding humor was of vital importance to him. "And it gives me a little insight into what's going on in your life," he added.

She wouldn't have thought he cared about what was happening in her life. "Does that matter?"

He shrugged casually. He didn't want to admit too much, not when she hadn't said anything yet about her feelings. Otherwise, the balance would be completely off. "Well, we're friends. Kind of."

Yes, they were, she thought. Maybe they really had been all along. Feeling magnanimous, she decided to let him in on a secret. "You're the reason the strip exists, you know."

He didn't see the connection. "Me?"

"Yes." Eager, warming to her subject, Traci moved closer to him. "Don't you remember? I used to draw a little figure on the bottom of my Christmas envelopes, waving goodbye."

"That's right." He did remember that—a tiny, quick little sketch that bore only a slight resemblance to the familiar figure that graced his breakfast table every morning.

"You said it would be interesting to see what she was capable of doing besides waving. So I took it a step further—"

That was putting it mildly. He hadn't thought of Traci as capable of modesty. But then, he hadn't thought she was capable of burning his socks off with a single kiss, either.

"A very big step. You've got calendars and T-shirts and Christmas cards—"

The way he was rattling off the litany surprised her. "How do you know that?"

He laughed shortly. "Hard not to when it's staring you in the face everywhere you go."

Traci knew better. He wasn't getting off that easily. "Not if you don't go where they're sold."

She had him there. He had been following the development of her creation with more than just passing interest. "I suppose not."

Traci tucked her feet under her on the sofa, settling in like a squatter. "So you have all this insight into me and I don't really have any into you." She cocked her head, her eyes holding his. "Don't you think you should reciprocate?"

"No." He didn't like talking about himself. His job, his career choice, was to listen and to plead other people's causes, not his own.

"C'mon, tell me something about you." His reticence reminded her of the old Morgan. She tugged on his shirtsleeve. "How did you go from a skinny guy to a muscular backwoodsman who practices law on the side?" Her own words evoked a girlhood image in her mind. "Hey, that sounds a little like Lincoln." She considered that. "Except he wasn't so muscular."

Only she would reach for a comparison that far off. He thought for a moment. "I guess you're partly to blame for that."

Traci blinked, surprised. "Me?" She'd never made any suggestions to him, not ones that were constructive at any rate.

"Yes." He grinned as he saw the confusion in her eyes. She really did have a hand in his decision, though he hadn't realized it consciously until now. "I figured arguing with you every summer put me in fighting condition to plead cases before juries."

Was it her imagination, or did he look even better by firelight? The golden glow from the hearth bathed his skin in deep, tanned hues. Just looking at him had her stomach muscles tightening until they were taut, like the head of a drum.

She was more interested in the other aspect. "And the backwoodsman part?"

That was even simpler to trace. "I started working out the fall right after you knocked out my tooth."

Traci frowned. "I thought we settled all that yesterday. You knocked out your own tooth."

Morgan wasn't about to concede that so easily. "Which I wouldn't have done if you hadn't punched me in the stomach," he reminded her.

She grinned, amused. "You're right, you were destined to become a lawyer." She paused, her eyes skimming along the ridges of muscles that were firm and hard, even though they were relaxed. "So these are mine, huh?"

He wasn't quite sure what she was driving at. "What?"

Lightly, she ran the tip of her finger along his biceps. "Well, you just said you wouldn't have started working out if it wasn't for me, so I guess that makes me partially responsible for them. Translated, that makes them mine."

He laughed as he shook his head in wonder. "I've never met anyone who thinks the way you do. Do you realize that your thought process is so scrambled that it seems to work almost sideways?'' That was the best description for it he could come up with.

The light in his eyes warmed her. As did his smile. If she were a cat, she thought, she'd be purring right now. "That's what makes me unique.''

He inclined his head. "If you say so." Morgan paused. She didn't shift her gaze. "You're staring."

She was, she realized. Caught, she averted her eyes and looked into the fire. "Sorry, just thinking."

He'd embarrassed her, he thought. Curiosity aroused, he prodded. "About?"

No way was she about to tell him that she was wondering how those arms would feel around her just now. He could torture her and she wouldn't admit it. At least, not without his giving up a piece of himself first.

Traci waved her hand vaguely. "Just that I can't wait for tomorrow, when this nightmare is finally over."

Her choice of words didn't exactly please him. Morgan studied her face. "This has been a nightmare for you?"

Instead of answering, she asked, "Do you like being stranded like this?"

His eyes skimmed lightly over her face. "That depends on who I'm stranded with."

He couldn't be thinking what she thought he

was thinking. Nervously, she cleared her throat. "My point exactly. You probably can't wait to get back to the city." Holding her breath, she watched his face for a reaction.

"Oh, I think I can wait."

When he looked at her like that, she could almost feel his touch. Her breath caught in her throat, refusing to budge. "You mean you don't like your work?"

He smiled slowly as he began to toy with a button on her shirt. "I like my work very much, but I wasn't thinking about that just now."

Breathe, Traci, breathe. She forced oxygen into her lungs—and felt light-headed. "What were you thinking about?"

The smile had worked its way into his eyes. And her soul. "Guess."

She'd never been a coward before. But she was afraid to guess. Afraid of being wrong and looking foolish. "Morgan, you're beginning to scare me."

This was something new, a Traci who wasn't sure of herself. "Why, Traci?" he asked softly, his breath whispering along the planes of her face. "Why am I beginning to scare you?"

She wet her lips. They seemed to dry instantly. "Well, maybe because I'm having the same kinds of thoughts that you are—and I shouldn't be. I mean, this is us. You and me." And it was so improbable.

Wasn't it?

"Yes." He pressed a soft, small kiss to her temple, instantly melting her. "It is."

It was hard to talk when her tongue refused to move. "We're not supposed to feel—understand?" She couldn't make it come out any clearer than that. She felt completely inept.

"Probably, but right now, I am." Very lightly, he feathered kisses along her forehead, even around the bandage. He felt rather than heard Traci moan. "I'm feeling a whole host of things that are confusing the hell out of me."

At least he was being honest. But then, this was Morgan. He would always be honest. That much she knew about him. It meant a lot.

"Like?"

"Like wondering what it would be like to kiss you again." Deliberately, he avoided her mouth as he wove the wreath of kisses along her face. He was driving them both crazy. "Wondering what it would be like to hold you against me and feel your heart beating." His hands slid down along her arms, his eyes holding her prisoner. "Wondering what it would be like to make love with you."

She really wished he hadn't said that. It sliced apart the last of her resistance.

"You, too, huh?"

He felt as if he were looking into her soul and it was a mirror of his own. "Meaning you've thought about it, too?"

She couldn't give him that. It was too much. "No, I've tried not to think about it."

He grinned, his mouth grazing the side of her temple again. She could feel his smile seeping into her skin. "There's that sideways thinking again."

Deftly, he worked his way down to the next button, removing it from the hole even more slowly than he had the first one.

She felt herself sinking into an almost drugged state. Drugged and energized at the same time. How was that possible? "Crops up every time you're around." Every word was an effort for her.

"I doubt that." She probably thought like that all the time, he mused. He was beginning to get accustomed to it. And like it.

"Don't." When he stopped, his fingers releasing the button he'd been teasing out of its hole, Traci placed her hands over his and guided him back to what he was doing. "I meant 'don't doubt it,' not 'don't do it.'"

Two buttons were released. His fingers tugged on a third. "Then you want me to?"

She didn't ask what. She didn't have to. She merely nodded.

"That's good. That's very good." Because if she'd asked him to stop, he wasn't certain he could, not without sacrificing a chunk of himself in the process.

Very slowly, he removed the rest of the buttons from their holes. All the while, his gaze was fixed on hers. He saw the excitement leap to her eyes as his fingers skimmed along the outline of her breast. It fed his own.

"You know, if you were wearing my shirt, this would go a lot faster."

"You don't like fast." It wasn't a guess. She *knew*. "If you did, you would have had this off me by now."

She was right. He smiled as he slid the material down her bare shoulders, anointing each first with a kiss. "Complaining?"

"Noticing." Nerves jumping, she bit her lip. "Being afraid."

He didn't want her to be afraid, not of this. Not of him. "Of what?"

She took a deep breath and let it out. "That I'll get enough courage to make you stop." His hands stilled for a moment. "Or that you will stop."

Only Traci. His thumb teased the clasp at her back. "Can't have it both ways, Traci."

The bra slipped away from her breasts like a queen's servant bowing his way out of a room. Her skin tingled as the cool air came in contact with it. Traci fell into his arms, pressing herself against him, her mouth sealing to his.

"Yes, I can," she breathed. "Don't tell me what I can do."

"Wouldn't dream of it," Morgan murmured against her mouth. She was a constant source of surprise to him. A mystery box that defied opening.

But he was bent on trying.

His hands were hot upon her body, hotter than any flame could ever be, she thought. Excitement leapt so high within her that it made her dizzy.

And everywhere he touched her, everywhere he brushed against her, was singed. Pulses were vibrating all along her body, anticipation within her mounted with every pass of his fingers, every movement of his hands.

Every promise he silently made her.

Eager to bring her flesh to his, Traci began taking off his shirt. She felt several buttons loosen as she mimicked his actions.

And in between, they kissed. Kissed so that both were completely numb, operating on automatic pilot and needs that were far greater than any sense of order or logic could ever be.

She wanted him. She wanted him more than she'd ever wanted anyone before. More, she knew, than she would ever want anyone again.

Except for him.

Guilt rose, distant, but hoary, to torment her. She struggled against it.

"We shouldn't be doing this," she breathed against his mouth.

She didn't mean it, he thought. But what if she did? "Want me to stop?"

No! She fairly whimpered. The very thought of his stopping now weakened her knees. "If you do, I'll be forced to kill you."

The laugh in his throat was deep, sensual. Almost primal. "Wouldn't want that."

She stopped a moment, her lips blurred from racing along his face, and looked at him. "No, but I do want you. Am I crazy?"

"Probably," he guessed, framing her face so

that he could kiss her again. "But so am I." He couldn't get enough, never enough. The more he kissed her, the more he wanted to kiss her. The more he felt her body rub along his, the more he wanted that body. "Traci, you turn everything inside out, including me."

He wasn't the only one. "There's a lot of that going around," she murmured.

Nude, with their clothes tangled in a hopeless heap, Traci and Morgan reveled in an exploration of tastes, textures and contours.

Nothing was left untouched. Most especially not their hearts.

Morgan gathered her close to him, his mouth drawing in sustenance from hers. And while he sealed his lips, his very soul, to her, his hands took possession of what already had been declared his.

It humbled him. She was soft to the touch. Soft and giving and incredibly silken. She seemed to pour through his hands like a precious life force. The image of that laughing-eyed girl melted away in the heat of the passion generated by the ripe woman who twisted so urgently beneath his hands.

Needs pounded against him. Morgan wanted to rush, to claim what he knew was waiting there for him. But he forced himself to take it slow, to give her every bit of her due.

And to imprint this night indelibly on both their minds.

For he wasn't about to let her return to Donald

or Daniel or whatever the hell his name was, with her heart intact. Not after tonight. Not after he'd had her like this. And not after she'd had him.

Drunk, she was completely drunk, Traci realized. Far more drunk than she'd been on the wine last night. Drunk and empowered at the same time.

Whatever he was doing to her was making her feel as if she were having an out-of-body experience. She delighted in his expertise on a dual level, both joining him and yet standing back and taking a reckoning of what was happening to her. To them. She wasn't a novice, but this was an entirely new level of pleasure for her.

Morgan? This was Morgan? When had he learned to be all things to her? To make her want to sob in sheer ecstasy even as she scrambled to grab a little more of the pleasure he was doling out to her so freely.

Had she somehow missed all the signs? Or was this something he'd acquired of late? From Cynthia?

Jealousy reared and then disappeared in the same instant. It didn't matter what had come before. All that mattered was this moment, now.

With him.

Traci grasped his shoulder, tempted to bite down hard as his mouth seared her breast. She twisted and turned, eager to absorb more, as he trailed his lips along her body, grazing, teasing.

He was making things happen to her she'd

never thought possible. Anticipation rippled through her like a lightning bolt creasing the sky. She didn't know if she could take much more of this.

"Where in the world did you learn to do that?" she gasped. Morgan raised himself back up to her level. She wasn't sure if she could move anymore.

"Instinct." He smiled into her eyes. "Pure instinct."

If there was a quip for this, she wasn't capable of mustering it, not now. All she could do was raise her head slightly as she knotted her arms around his neck. With the last bit of energy she had, Traci brought his face down to hers.

"There's something to be said for that," she whispered just before she kissed him. Draining him. Draining herself.

And then he was over her, claiming her the way her body begged to be claimed. The way he'd wanted to from the moment he'd seen her standing outside the house on Friday.

Slipping into her, Morgan could feel her heart hammering hard against his chest. Very slowly, he began to move. She moaned, then joined in, mimicking him. The intensity grew as journey's end approached.

The rhythm they achieved was echoed by the pounding of both their hearts. They rode out the storm they had created until it crested. Exhausted, they slid down the mountainside together, still locked in an embrace.

It seemed an eternity before his head finally

cleared. Morgan turned his face toward hers and looked down. He was just barely balancing his weight, trying not to crush her beneath him, although the temptation was there. He wouldn't mind being sealed to her for all time.

"That was you, wasn't it?"

She let out a long, contented sigh, her eyes still closed. "I think so."

"Maybe I'd better check." He shifted a little. "Any distinguishing moles or scars?"

It took her a moment to gather enough breath to answer. "Just the tire marks over my body that you left behind when you ran over it just now." Traci opened her eyes and looked up at him in unabashed awe. "Morgan, you do have hidden talents."

He nibbled on her lower lip. "Just takes the right person to bring them out."

And that would be her, she thought, secretly hugging the comment to her. "That *is* a compliment."

The time for games was over. At least for now. "Yes, I know." Shifting, Morgan lay back on the floor. He tucked his arm around her shoulders and nestled her against him. "Next time, we have to try it on a bed."

"Next time?" She didn't know whether to laugh or to cry. Or what to make of either reaction.

"Next time," he repeated firmly.

Hope skipped through her. "Then this isn't a one-night stand?"

He wasn't that kind of a man. He never had been. "Not in my book."

Guilt rose again, insistent and annoying. "I'm supposed to be engaged."

He wasn't about to let her wheedle out of this. She cared about him. He knew that, had felt that. There were no more secrets, not after tonight. "No, you were thinking about whether or not to be engaged. And I think you came to a decision."

"I did?" She tried to sound flippant, but couldn't quite manage to carry it off.

He shifted her so that she was over him. "Let me refresh your memory."

"Oh." Startled, she realized what she'd just felt beneath her. A grin burst out, lighting her eyes. "Okay."

10

Hazy with sleep and the rosy contentment that came from a night of lovemaking, Morgan reached for Traci before he even opened his eyes.

His hand came in contact with her hair. The vague thought drifted across his mind that she must have slid down to waist level on the pallet they'd formed out of blankets on the floor.

He didn't remember her hair feeling so coarse. Or being so short.

When she growled, his eyes flew open. Morgan sucked in his breath before the image looming over him stabilized into a mass of fur, hot breath and dripping tongue. It was Jeremiah.

The sound of Traci's laughter surrounded him. This would be her idea of a joke. Sitting up, Morgan uttered a good-humored oath as he dragged his hand through his tousled hair. He was feeling too good to be annoyed.

"You're up."

Traci had thrown on her clothes and was sitting cross-legged on the floor not far from him, sketching. She'd felt inspired this morning. Things were finally coming together for her. It showed in her work.

"Uh-huh." She glanced at her watch. "I've been up for about half an hour." She nodded toward the kitchen. "The phone's working."

Suspicions began to nudge at him. He studied her profile. "How would you know that?"

Traci put the finishing touches on the middle panel. She liked to complete each before going on to the next. This one was shaping up rather well, even if she did say so herself.

"I made a call." Her answer was distracted as she plotted the next frame.

Why was there this odd, unsettled feeling in the pit of his stomach? As if he were waiting to find out if he was going to be wheeled into the operating room, or released from the hospital with a clean bill of health?

"Oh?" He tried to sound disinterested. But he wasn't. He was very interested in whom she had placed the call to. "To a garage in town?"

"No, to Daniel in his hotel in Connecticut." Two figures began to take shape in the last panel. She smiled. She had a feeling that Mike the VCR repairman was going to be a new regular in *Traci on the Spot*. "I told him I had to see him once he got back."

So it was business as usual. And last night had meant nothing. Morgan's jaw hardened. He glanced down at the sheet that was haphazardly sprawled out over his lower extremities, just barely covering the essentials.

"Do you think you should be telling me this while I'm lying here, naked?" He looked around. Damn, where were his clothes, anyway? The dog had probably buried them. He wouldn't put it past the mutt. After all, it was her dog.

"I don't know, should I?" Calling Daniel at the hotel had been one of the hardest calls she'd ever made. And the worst was yet ahead. But it had to be done. Her voice grew quiet. "I told him we had to talk about getting engaged."

"Then you are?" He had to hear her say it, say that last night hadn't meant anything to her. Say that she was marrying Daniel, anyway. Then maybe this sinking feeling would leave.

"No, we're not." She set the sketch pad aside

and looked at Morgan. Why was he so surprised? Didn't he realize that she couldn't have made love with him if her heart belonged to someone else? "I want to tell him in person that I can't be engaged to him and emotionally involved with—" Morgan was looking at her so expectantly she just couldn't bring herself to say it. "Well, I just can't get engaged, that's all."

He moved closer to her. He needed to hear the words. "Why?"

He was going to make this difficult, wasn't he? Why wasn't she surprised? Traci blew out a breath. She might as well recite her reasons.

"Because you showed me that the bells and the banjos are too important to me to leave out. That, ultimately, I won't be happy without them." Traci looked at his face and saw Morgan for perhaps the first time. Her heart skipped a little beat. Damn, that was the face of the man she wanted. The man she loved. But she probably couldn't get him, last night notwithstanding. "That they still do exist for me and that I shouldn't sell out before I find them."

Morgan frowned. "I think you've lost me here. Didn't you just say that you'd found them?" *With me,* he added silently.

"Yes, that's what I said." Traci discovered that her patience this morning was very short and raw. "But that was with you."

He didn't see the problem. "And—?"

She hated having to spell out everything like this. "Well, you don't want a relationship." She slanted a look at him and prayed that it didn't appear as hopeful as she felt. "Do you?"

She was a puzzlement, there was no disputing that. "What made you think I didn't?"

She laughed shortly. "Ten years of coming up here each summer for openers."

He took this slowly, one step at a time. Love wasn't ordinarily something you jumped into, although he certainly seemed to have. Somewhere in the middle of the night, it had hit him. And he rather liked the impact. He was in love with Traci and was willing to allow that maybe a part of him in some small way always had been.

Otherwise, why would he have felt so compelled to orchestrate all this?

"I grant you that the twelve-year-old boy I was didn't want any sort of a relationship—on any level—with the ten-year-old girl you were. But that's in the past. The distant past," he emphasized. "Last night is still palpitating."

Nervous, she ran the tip of her tongue along her lips. She saw desire bloom in his eyes and it thrilled her. And gave her hope. "And you think last night is the basis for starting something?"

Was she being deliberately dense, or couldn't she see? He laughed. "Lady, haven't you noticed? It's already started. The train has left the station and you're in the head car."

Pressing her lips together, she managed to hold back her smile. "Who's the engineer?"

Arranging the sheet over himself, he sat back. "Guess."

She didn't have to. This was just like him. Never mind that she was beginning to really like what was just like him. "Why don't I get to be engineer?"

Just like old times, he thought fondly. But with one hell of a difference. "'Cause you're a girl and it was my idea."

Traci sniffed and pretended to look away disdainfully. "Sexist."

His mouth curved as he grabbed her and pulled her to him. She tumbled against him willingly. "Only when it comes to the things that count—like you."

She gloried in the feel of his body beside her. "I count?"

Morgan could only shake his head. "If you haven't figured that one out yet, you're not as bright as I always thought you were."

He lowered his mouth to hers, but she pushed him back. "You always thought I was bright?" This was certainly news to her.

Why did she look so surprised? "Sure."

He was just saying that to get on her good side now. "You never said anything."

"Of course I didn't," he admitted. "It was against the code."

Warm wisps of desire floated through her as he ran his hand along her arm. "What code?"

He pressed a kiss to her throat. "The male supremacist code."

He was making it awfully difficult to think. "And since when were you a supremacist?"

Morgan stopped and raised his head to look at her. "You mean you didn't notice?"

"No." She almost laughed the answer in his face.

He feigned disappointment. "Damn, I must have been doing something wrong."

Love softened her expression. "No, Morgan, I think you were doing everything right."

He rose, the sheet pooling to the floor at his feet. Damn, but he was a magnificent specimen of manhood, she thought. And as unselfconscious about it as the day he was born.

Morgan took her hand in his and turned toward the stairs. "Why don't we go upstairs to your bedroom where we can discuss this further?"

Traci let herself be led off willingly, but she glanced at the phone as they passed. "Before we call the towing service?"

He was gently tugging her up the stairs. "Way before."

Humor and desire vied for the same space. "Don't you want to be rescued?"

"No." Morgan's hand tightened around hers. "Not particularly."

She could feel her heart begin to race. "You know what?"

At the landing Morgan turned to look at her. He hadn't known it was possible to want someone so much. And he had a feeling he hadn't even begun to scratch the surface. "What?"

"Neither do I."

He took her into his arms, unable to wait. His

mouth found hers and did incredible things to the composition of her body, turning it to hot liquid. It melted in the heat coming from his hard, lean body.

"Knew we'd find common ground if we looked hard enough." Taking her hand again, Morgan guided her to her room.

"Morgan?"

He looked at her. Was she hesitating? No, he didn't think so. "Hmm?"

Doubts and anticipations nibbled at her. "Do you think it'll work between us?" She'd never wanted anything to succeed so much in her life.

The woman talked way too much. "Damned if I know." He began unbuttoning her shirt, just as slowly as he had last night. "But I think it's worth a shot."

She could feel her breath catching in her throat. "How long?"

"The first hundred years ought to do it." The shirt hung open at her sides. He noticed with satisfaction that she hadn't bothered putting on her bra. He rather liked this style. Morgan slid his hands beneath her blouse, cupping her breasts. "After that, you get your walking papers."

She raised her chin, her eyes dancing. "No, you get yours."

He pretended to take that into consideration. "We'll work out the fine print later."

Traci laughed. "Deal. You know, I think I *am* going to buy this house from your parents, after all."

"Sorry, it's not for sale."

Her eyes narrowed. "But you said—"

Morgan smiled at her. "I lied."

She didn't understand. It didn't make any sense. "Why?"

"Because I picked up the paper last week and read *Traci on the Spot*. Suddenly, I knew I had to see you before you became officially engaged."

"Why?" she pressed.

It was the same question he'd asked himself. Over and over again. "That I didn't know." He drew her even closer. "Until now. I guess, subconsciously, maybe I always knew that you and I were meant to be." He grinned. "Either that, or I was a hell of a masochist."

It was hard carrying on a sensible conversation with a nude man. Not when she wanted him so much. Anticipation was growing to phenomenal proportions within her. Traci glanced meaningfully toward her bed.

"About those negotiations…?"

He laughed. It was going to be a damn good life. And they were going to make their mothers very happy women. "Ready when you are."

Traci laced her arms around his neck and pressed her body against his. "I'm always ready—when it comes to you."

"I'm very glad to hear that." He picked her up into his arms. Turning to enter the room, he saw that the dog was about to follow them. "Sorry, dog. These negotiations are going to be held in private.'' With the heel of his foot, Morgan closed the door behind him.

With what seemed to pass for a loud sigh, Jeremiah laid down before the bedroom, settling in as if he sensed that it was going to be a long time before the door was opened again.

* * * * *

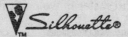